Henry, Henry

Henry, Henry

Brian Willems

Winchester, UK
Washington, USA

First published by Zero Books, 2017
Zero Books is an imprint of John Hunt Publishing Ltd., Laurel House, Station Approach,
Alresford, Hants, SO24 9JH, UK
office1@jhpbooks.net
www.johnhuntpublishing.com
www.zero-books.net

For distributor details and how to order please visit the 'Ordering' section on our website.

Text copyright: Brian Willems 2016

ISBN: 978 1 78535 547 9
978 1 78535 548 6 (ebook)
Library of Congress Control Number: 2016944520

A CIP catalogue record for this book is available from the British Library.

Design: Stuart Davies

Printed and bound by CPI Group (UK) Ltd, Croydon, CR0 4YY, UK

We operate a distinctive and ethical publishing philosophy in all
areas of our business, from our global network of authors to
production and worldwide distribution.

CONTENTS

To Jasna

Part One

CAPTAIN COOKE LED HENRY DOWN a spiral stone staircase underneath the performance hall. The bottom of the staircase opened into an octagonal room with two doors, one green and one blue. "Pick one," the Captain said, tightening his grip on Henry's arm.

"I don't understand," said Henry.

"What's not to understand?" answered the Captain, "It's easy. An easy task, let's call it. Just give us your favourite colour. Green or blue?"

Henry winced at the Captain's grip. "Then green. I guess green's my favourite colour."

In place of an answer the Captain looked down at Henry, waiting for him to move toward the green door. But Henry just stared back. "Now listen here, choirboy," the Captain said, "You've made your choice, so now take action. Just open the damn green door, and the faster you go through, the better it'll be for you."

Henry's eyes grew big and the rest of his face went dark, as if building up to a scream. The Captain set a shushing index finger against Henry's mouth and, with effort at restraining his anger, calmly whispered, "Get on with it, Henry. Or I'll shove you through the blue door, and you wouldn't want that, now would you?" Henry shook his head, taking the Captain's lingering finger back and forth with him. Then the Captain pulled his hand back slowly and Henry walked to the green door and stood in front of it. "Be a good boy," said the Captain, grinning.

Henry put his right hand, gloved in red Spanish silk, flat against a door made of planks roughly painted green. The Captain kicked him in the small of the back with his boot. Henry fell down on his knees. Then he slowly removed both gloves and tucked them together into the front of his belt, stood up, opened the green door, and went in.

"HERE, I'VE BROUGHT YOU THIS," said Martino. He was Henry's first visitor, best friend, and a number of years older. He handed Henry a clean and fragrant white shirt. Martino found Henry in rather good spirits despite being incarcerated in a windowless pitch-black room not much bigger than a body stretched outright. Henry was on his feet, leaning against the far wall. Martino was required to leave the door open while visiting, and the faint light from outside uncovered Henry's soiled britches. Henry had at some point taken off his shirt and bundled it carelessly on the floor in a corner. He had been there for a week.

"Thank you," said Henry, but he refused to take the fresh shirt. "Show it to me," he said.

Martino unfolded the shirt and caught a piece of ginger root as it fell out.

"Oh, God," said Henry, his eyes adjusting to the light, "that's just splendid." The scent of the ginger began to overtake the depression of the cell.

"Just a second," said Martino, and he searched the cell walls with his hand for a crook in which to stick the root. "My Auntie packed this. It's ginger, to freshen the clothes. Plus it helps the stomach. My stomach, anyway. I have stomach aches," he said. "Just like you. It'll help." Martino wedged the ginger into the top of a half-pried door hinge.

"There," Martino said, "now turn over there." Henry turned away as Martino unfurled the clean shirt, blew air into the sleeves, and slid it over Henry's shoulders. "Button it yourself, though," said Martino, but Henry did not move. "In the front," Martino suggested. Then Henry slowly turned back around and buttoned the shirt, getting all the buttons matched right the first time because he had a musician's fingers, and a musician's fingers can do a lot, even in the dark. Then, as Henry started to experience having a clean shirt on again, and as Martino heard the jail keeper loudly making his way down the stairs to let Martino and Henry know that their time was up, Henry thought he could smell a mix of apples in the cloth, commingling with the ginger. It made Henry retch all over his chest. He took the shirt off before he was finished throwing up. However, he would not give it back to Martino, no matter how many times his friend asked before being led out of the cell by the keeper.

TWO WEEKS LATER the Captain brought Henry back up the staircase, through the kitchen, and out into the courtyard. Henry knew he was about to be introduced to what the choirboys privately called "the services." This was the year 1673, when out of 120 sentences for criminal behaviour handed out by the Royal Court, 113 entailed the death penalty. The death penalty could be carried out in a variety of manners: hanged until dead, strangled and broken, broken until dead, drawn by four horses, head cut off, head broken, strangled then burnt, broken alive, dying on the wheel.

The Captain was a man of many talents. He not only fulfilled his role as master of the Chapel Royal choir, but, due to his vast battlefield experience in the Civil War, was concurrently employed as the manager of "the services." In other words, the Captain was also assistant penal administrator to the crown, which means he had to clean up the messes the punishments of the crown tended to create. The Captain was in charge of tidying the gallows, racks, tools and other equipment of justice. It was in this capacity that he combined choir and shackle. When a boy misbehaved he first served an indeterminate amount of time in either the green or the blue room, which were both the same, door colours aside. There one would "focus attention on things past, things present, and things to come," as the Captain would say. Then the miscreant would be thrust neck-high into the muck of jurisprudence. This would wipe the offender's mind clean of any thought of landing back in the position of criminal again. The length of time a choirboy spent in either the green or the blue room would vary, since capital punishment kept no timetable. Some lockdowns lasted mere hours, while others lasted weeks. Each boy was instructed to keep silent about the affair, an order which not a single boy obeyed.

Henry watched a man being half-led, half-dragged out into the courtyard. Since Henry had to hold position near the gallows, the prisoner was led right toward him. Henry started to sweat from the proximity, realizing that he was also going to have a role to play in the active portion of this person's life.

The criminal was brought up to Henry by two men, one on either side. He was presented, as if for inspection.

"Well?" asked the first man. Henry did not know what to say.

The first man looked at the second, who said, "Typical. Another pansy boy properly prepared for his duty, I see." Then they dropped the man down at Henry's feet and walked back the way they came.

Henry looked around the courtyard, anywhere but at the man on the ground, lying too close to his feet. Eventually he spied the Captain leaning on his balcony, grinning down at his choirboy's discomfort. The Captain then looked at the criminal before turning back to Henry. The only instruction he communicated was to gesture to Henry to get on with it. "Oh, Jesus," Henry said. Then he closed his eyes and bent down to pick up the criminal. He was helped by complete compliance from the man at his feet. At the sudden easement of his task Henry opened his eyes and led the man up to the gallows. The crowd which had been forming started to laugh, although Henry did not notice it because as he reached the gallows he found himself eye-to-eye with the condemned man, who began to speak rather eloquently for being so near the end.

"He thinks I'm a spy, the fool. Easier for me to be framed as betrayer of the crown than for him to admit that his wife is the whore all London knows her to be." Henry did not know what to do. The crowd started to move in closer. The criminal said, loud enough for one or two of the spectators to hear, "It was during dinner. The *Lady* of the house always enjoyed a smoke afterwards. As I was among their servants, it was my job to light the Lady's cheroot, which burst into flame. They do that. Something they add to the tobacco, they say. Even though I knew this I still started and ducked behind the Lady's chair. That was enough to be convicted. It was seen as a sign of intimacy with the woman. But there was more. Then I was accused of tying a traitorous message to a kestrel. They said I was sending plans of the planned British attack on a number of French coastal towns, and I was sentenced with the utmost haste. If only they knew the truth. About her." The criminal looked around at the crowd who had gathered closer to hear. "Although the fact that I find myself here is surely a sign that they do." He carried himself as if he were used to an audience, perhaps holding table with the servants. Then he looked up as if in supplication, but his eyes landed on the Captain. "Him! Dear Captain, Captain Cooke. What a wife. A *Lady*," the volume of his voice increasing, "*We know what a lady is!*"

But by the time he had finished his accusation Captain Cooke had already formulated his response. He stood up and moved to the edge of the balcony. He took in the gathering of spectators with a serious gaze and then said: "The gallows are too good for this swine. This traitor to the crown must not be hanged, but broken!"

Henry only vaguely knew what being broken entailed. After the guards brushed him aside and took the criminal down from the gallows he found out. It means that as many bones are broken as possible without killing, so that, after a while, when the victim can no longer really feel any more pain added on top of what he or she has already experienced, there remains only the snap of the bones to bring about an auditory awareness of the damage being done.

The criminal's lump of broken flesh was eventually spread across the raised platform of the gallows. The spectators had all gone home, or at least away. Perhaps they did not want to be reminded of the cheering and bonding in which they partook during the festival, for it was a festival, since there had been food, drink, music and dancing. Henry's work comprised of clearing away splinters of wood, ends of rope, snapped bones, and much-too-identifiable body parts. With the Captain's steady look burning down from his courtyard perch, Henry, for the first but not the last time in his life, started to haul what was left of a carcass onto the bed of a wood cart unattached to a horse. To attach such a cart to a horse would defile the animal for any other purpose. With people being more plentiful and hence more disposable than horses, Henry was tasked to pull the cart instead.

MASEY TRIED TO WIGGLE her back up the headboard. Meredith screamed. She hadn't seen her mother move more than a twitch of her facial features for over a week. Meredith hurried around behind the bed and gently pulled up the pillow by the two lace corners on its longer side, vicariously pulling up her mother as well. The pillowcase had been made by Meredith's grandmother. Now, the left corner peeping over the headboard, it cast a shadow, sent by a spirit lamp on a nightstand, across the bed, down onto the floor, and halfway up the wall to the window overlooking the front of the house. Masey could see no more than blue sky out the window. The elm that had grown on the northeast corner of the house, sending its branches across the bedroom window for mid-day shade, a shade Meredith's father called "God's gift to two p.m.," had been brutally trimmed three months prior in the hope of stopping Dutch-elm disease.

Therefore, from the perspective of the bed, there was only sky to
be seen. But Masey was not looking out of the window at the
moment. She was looking at her daughter.

"I have something to tell you, Mere," said Masey, her eyes
bulging out at the brevity and completeness, the accuracy and
directness, of her own easily pronounced statement. Her upper
lip curled and her head tilted slightly back in a sign of self-
congratulation. "I have something to tell you, Mere," she
repeated, as if trying on a second shoe to see if the pair fit. "It's
not me that's a hostage here, dear, it's you."

"Oh Mother!" Meredith said, and gave her mother a hug and
cried and patted her head before remembering she wasn't to do
that, it was too formal. So she straightened the covers as if now,
lucid, her Mother would criticize Meredith's upkeep, which she
wasn't.

"You are a hostage and a keeper of all my faults, and it is up
to you to correct this," Masey said.

"Please take it easy mother. Father will be home soon. So
please don't get too excited. Just take it slow."

"You just listen now, dear. Let me explain what I mean. I don't
know how long this will last. This… being here. Please listen and
don't think I'm crazy or it's the incision you think I don't know
about, or any such thing. It is me as much as it ever was me
walking in the garden or taking you to Lynes' for ices. You are a
hostage of my mistakes, and I want you to correct them. To
correct me, and soon. It will take the greatest attention on your
part, every step of every day, at least for a while. You will have to
keep all of my faults in mind, and not overdevelop a sense of how
good I was or think that I was a perfect mother just because I died
early or such rot. That kind of perfection kept in the heart of a
young girl will only lead her to unhappiness, and quite clearly
that is unacceptable. For you deserve a good life. You will have it
hard enough as it is, with your father, so you must do what I say.
A few days after my death," she patted the bed and Meredith sat

down, taking her mother's hand, "a few days after my death, make a list. A list of all my faults, everything I did wrong, how I scolded you when I shouldn't have. Like at the pool last month, for instance. Put down all the ways I wronged you: my lack of attention, how little time we spent together, the gross injustices I have perpetrated because I didn't make enough of an effort. It might sound strange to you now but it is very important. Here, I'll get you started." She let go of Meredith's hand. "Think of how I grounded you for a week for playing with Bobby Brighton. You were just playing, weren't you? I had no reason to react the way I did, but I did, and you should resent me for it. It's your right. That's item number one for your list. And you should add to it whenever you think of something new. When you think of something good about me, that's fine too. I hope you do. And often. But don't write it down. You'll need no encouragement in that area, being such a young girl. Make this list and keep it with you, in your purse or handbag, making sure you have a masterlist somewhere at home, in case your forget your purse or it is stolen. Especially if you go into town. Take that list and read it every day. That's really it. Nothing more should be required. Read the list daily and add to it occasionally. At least for a while. A year or two. It's the recipe for a good life. I know it sounds odd, but it's true, believe me. I once had a mother too." Meredith straightened the pillowcase behind her mother's head because she heard her father coming in.

"Oh father!" said Meredith, indicating her mother's state by clapping softly over her head. John stopped at the edge of the bed.

"John," said Masey. "Now the both of you, please ask what you will. Anything. And I will tell you what I can. Then you should get a good sleep tonight, for I feel you'll have more than your hands full with arrangements in the morning." And Masey, answering their questions briefly and directly, talked to them of what it was like to have an active mind unable to make itself apparent to the outside world, of burial plots and finances, of brothers and sisters and prayers. Then she sank back down into the mattress of the bed, bending the shadow cast by her pillowcase down even further.

THE FIRST TIME THAT Captain Cooke's wife Evelyn made contact with Henry was after a concert of pieces from Frederick Wolff, picked mainly to utilize the 24 violins Charles II had installed in the Royal Chapel under the influence of the French court, although he also added a section of cornets which had been dropped by the French two decades previous. During the concert, Henry found his stomach starting to spin. He thought he picked up the faint smell of apples. He looked up at Martino standing next to him, with a plea for help in his eyes. Martino shrugged his shoulders and slightly increased his vocal output, attempting to cover up for Henry. It was after this painful performance that Henry, putting away some of the choir's costumes backstage, nearly bumped into Evelyn.

"Pardon me, Mademoiselle Cooke," Henry said.

"No need, Henry my friend, no need," Evelyn said. "Having some trouble with your garment?" And in fact he was having trouble folding it right, for his musician hands had begun to tremble. Evelyn took the gown and started to fold it herself. "It must be a bit strange for a boy like you be taking care of the linen. I cannot imagine you did such a thing at home."

"No, Mademoiselle," he said, "I did not."

"That is what I thought. But do correct me if I am mistaken Henry. Not that I think that I am, for if I thought that I were I would not venture to say so. But nevertheless, if you find me in error, please have no hesitation to correct me."

"Error in what, Mademoiselle?"

"Error in all I have to say dear Henry. Error perhaps in what I have previously said. For example, in the statement regarding your duties at home. And the manner in which you were accustomed to living before you came to this swine heap."

"No, Mademoiselle. Not in error I mean. I mean, I have had to learn a lot of things here at the Chapel, things I could not have imagined before my arrival."

"A lot of things, Henry, such as?"

"Taking care of many different things."

"You mean the corpses, outside, in the courtyard, do you not?" She stopped folding the gown and held it close to her chest. "I am fairly sure, even more so than in my previous statement, that you never had to do anything quite like that before, is that right? How did it make you feel? You took care of the body of Monsieur Pauvre? Did you know he was innocent? Set up by the Captain because he had slipped one-too-many times into my bed? Once was tolerable, but it had been going on for months. Espionage! Ha! A message concealed in the foot of a falcon! Rubbish. Lies. But did you have any idea that such things could happen? Here in the Chapel, I mean? Such deceit? You must have, I am sure, or rather, I'm not so sure, now that I think about it. Meaning, now that I see this damn expression on your face."

"I do not quite understand, Mademoiselle," Henry said, distractedly, due to seeing William coming up behind them. Evelyn went quiet. William handed Henry another three gowns to put away. That was how news of the affair between Henry and Evelyn spread before it even began.

MEREDITH GOT MUCH MORE from her mother than a list. She got a shirt. A white shirt. A white shirt she wore only when her mother's birthday came around, which was April 6. And then she only wore it at home and then only for a few minutes; but she wore it. She wore it alone and unmarried and waiting in good humor. Her father had been dead for over four years. On this April 6 Meredith had a sore throat since she liked to keep the windows open for the cool air while she slept. So she had extra hot tea for breakfast.

This was in an apartment in Southwark. After her father's death she sold the house and bought something smaller, something in which she could live without much fuss. Meredith did like fuss, but not too much. She liked to clean but only occasionally. She liked to pack but only sparingly, for short trips with small, easy-to-carry luggage.

Meredith had to wear her mother's shirt for shorter than usual because she was going on holiday. When she unpacked her suitcase at her destination not an item was wrinkled, not a corner undone, even taking in consideration all of the heaving to the tops of luggage racks and mistreatment in the hands of well-meaning bellboys. The linen survived, Meredith thought, meaning it remained crisp. Meredith liked to pride herself on her cleanliness, although she did not spend much time on it. She was merely efficient. She did a good job at anything she started, and she did things in small batches, rather than saving them up for weeks, so that she actually felt pleasure in devoting so much energy to each and every crease in a shirt.

Meredith was feeling clean and well-rested on the beach at St Marcouf, on the coast of France, where a number of the English had gathered to ride out the summer in relative comfort. She reached into her wicker bag, next to her lounge-chair, and, without looking, fingered the list of her Mother's mistakes.

But she was not really thinking about her mother. She had been looking down at a certain spot on the sand without realizing it: a hermit crab between homes.

THE SECOND TIME EVELYN and Henry slept together Evelyn stroked Henry's forehead, cupped his balls, parted his hair, tickled his ribs, filled his pipe, pushed him off her, licked his ear and parted his toes with hers. In reply, Henry circled her nipples, ate some cheese, peeled an apple, played with himself, rolled over on his side, pulled up the covers, and all at once came up with the first three bars of his very first composition, *Sweet Tyranness, I Now Resign.*

ALMOST AS SOON AS the affair began it was interrupted. Captain Cooke burst into the choirboys' bedchamber to talk to Henry. Henry was sitting on his bed, talking to Martino.

"Martino," said Captain Cooke, "leave."

Martino left. Henry stood up.

"Sit down Henry." Henry did. "And I will sit down right here next to you." And Captain Cooke did, stretching out his clasped hands at the same time. He first crossed and then uncrossed his legs before pumping his arms back and forth twice and then standing back up. "I don't want to have to say this to you, Henry. You know now I respect your family, musicians all, and I have come to respect you, despite our previous differences."

"I understand, Captain."

"You learned about what you call our 'services,' and I dare say I have never yet had a repeat offender. At least not until now, not until you."

Henry stood up in a hurry and declared, "I won't lie to you, I'll admit it all if you want me to. Let's just get it done with, please."

"What do you mean, get it done with? You think this is something that will be over, ever? That this is something for which you can be punished and which we can then nicely forget? You think that there is some kind of light at the end of your tunnel? Well there's not!" the Captain yelled as he started to violently rummage through the things Henry stored under his bed in a box soiled by the dust and dirt which fell from the bottom of the mattress. The Captain sneezed. "My God, boy," he said, as he pulled some cloth out of the box. A swatch of the bastard scarlet Henry wore for his first performance at the Chapel. There were also three pairs of shoes, two of which Henry had never worn in front of the other choirboys less fortunate, which meant that he had never worn them at all at the Chapel, for almost all the choirboys were less well-off than he. The box also included three pairs of thigh stockings, two gray and one black, one banded hat, two extra bands, and one pair of cuffs. In addition there was a piece of ribbon for tidying up garters and shoestrings, a present from Evelyn upon one of his evening's departures. "Quite a collection you have here Henry. The son of a real gentleman, I see. Prim to the tip of your nose, I might say. And what purpose do these fineries serve your fellows? Where is your feeling for other men? Do you have no sense of charity, Henry? That is what I am asking you. Where is your sense of charity?"

Henry looked down at the floor, unsure of what was going on. "I wouldn't know, sir."

"Perfect Henry, perfect. You horde and you hide but it will get you nowhere. I have heard reports of this box, and now I see for myself the kind of boy you are. Do you know where this will send you? Back to services. Right back. A boy like you holding out on us. It's disgusting. It's really beneath you, Henry. And you shall get no light duty this time, no one-off and then back up to the warm Chapel with the rest of them." The Captain took a breath and looked around the empty boys' room, gathering strength. "This time it's going to be too much for you Henry, too much. I can feel it. A delicate boy like you, so in touch with his spirit. Little Henry with the balls to start composing his own music while the rest are at cards and worse. Henry blue balls thinking he can best the rest of us here in Chapel! You think we haven't noticed? Well we have, Henry. I have. I have noticed quite a bit, and I think it is time for you to take notice as well. Hoarding finery, composing music without permission. Lord knows what else. Back downstairs with you, green door or blue, it matters not.

Now! Get out of my sight!" Just as Henry began to wonder if the Captain was really that blind, or was just making up an excuse to punish him like he had with Pauvre, someone else came up behind him, knocked him out, and dragged him out of the room.

MARTINO SNEAKED AND BRIBED his way downstairs to see Henry. It was a month and a half after the beginning of his second incarceration. It was the green room again. Henry had noticed that much while being led collar-first by the Captain's new right-hand man, Albanus. Henry had a dim memory of hanging from a clenched fist while Albanus fished around for his keys to the room. The search for the keys was not a quick one, for Albanus was a Swede: he searched all the pockets, flaps and pouches he had on him without gain. He had almost given up before he struck upon the idea to hop up and down, lightly at first, and then with more vigour, without letting go of Henry. This hopping produced the desired jingle, which ended up coming from his vest pocket, upper-right-hand side. Once the key was located Henry also found himself coming into direct contact with the door, for Albanus, not known for his light touch, did not fail to strike Henry's head against the open door while dragging him into the cell in which he was to become, once again, prisoner.

"How is she?" Henry asked, feeling Martino's presence as much as hearing the door open and close, a sound he could hardly recognize since he had not heard it for so long. "How is she?" he asked again quickly.

"How is who?" Martino asked.

"Evelyn, Mademoiselle Cooke, how is she holding on? What has he done to her, the bastard! Tell me, friend, if that is what you still are. What has become of my sweet Evelyn?"

"Sorry Henry, but I have no idea how she is. She spends almost no time at all in Chapel, and when she does, she is rather busy with just about everyone else but us choirboys. Although to hear some of the stories Wood and Hartz have told, she is no real stranger to the choir room either. Although what can you really believe, boys being boys and all that?"

"So she is alive. But of course she is, because I am. We have escaped punishment. Or the real punishment. Our punishment. I have imagined so much but never that she was simply alright. I have nowhere to go, nowhere to think."

"Then let me help you. Here are some grapes, if you want them. Already peeled. They are supposed to be easier on the stomach, peeled."

Ignoring the work Martino did on the fruit, Henry said, "So Evelyn is alright. Then why am I here, Martino, can you tell me that? It cannot be the clothes. Or just them. I mean, is that really all there is?"

"Yes," said Martino, "you are here because of your wardrobe. The Captain is terribly jealous. Oh, and the cornets. The Captain keeps saying you've stolen all the cornets."

Henry sat on the floor of his cell. Cornets? Just because they had been brought to court as a filler in the treble range, since falsetto choirboys had been scarce, the cornets had got a bad reputation, being connected with the scarcity of good singers rather than as magnificent instruments in their own right, able to hold their own next to any trumpet or other brass instrument. But steal them? Henry could never. So this was a false punishment. But at the same time, hopefully, it was the real one. Although Pauvre had been framed for treason, maybe Henry was believed really to be a thief.

But his personal fate was not the real question for Henry. His foremost concern was what was going on with Evelyn and Wood. Or with Hartz for that matter. And who had stolen the cornets anyway? Unless they were one and the same person, Evelyn's new flame and the cause of Henry's current state of respite mixed with despair. Henry could not stand it, and now even this all-too-short visit from Martino, a visit still in progress, was suspect.

Why had Martino told him about the cornets? Was the remark innocent or sly? Maybe Martino's visit was a set-up, a trap, a staged act, a play that was being written by the Captain. But maybe Evelyn was in on it too. Pauvre had been a "skilled" lover, she had said. But maybe she had just been looking for an easy way out of a tiresome liaison, inventing the rumour of treason herself?

Henry tried to continue speaking with Martino but he could not. He knew when he started speaking that his voice would betray his suspicion. He knew what he was going to say but he did not know how his words would betray him. He was going to say, "Martino, thank you for coming. You are a good friend." He had it planned already. But he was just too tired to get the words out.

What made it easier was that they were in the dark. Maybe Henry would die before he could say anything. Maybe he would expire right here on the floor of the cell, from hunger, stomach ulcer, dysentery, TB, love sickness, or melancholy. Could he die? It seemed like an easy question outside of the cell, but here, inside, it was not so simple. Henry was no longer even sure it was possible. He tried to see some light in the darkness of the cell, any kind of light, maybe something he had missed before, but he could see nothing. Then Henry looked even deeper into the centre of the cell. He felt his stomach drop when he saw, reflecting light coming from a place unknown, a glimmer on one of Martino's front teeth, for he had just opened his mouth to speak.

"WHEN SCHUBERT WAS DYING, he asked to be read *The Last of the Mohicans*, which he was, dutifully over the last five nights of his life, read by his wife. In my idle moments I hope they never reached the point where Le Renard Subtil falls at the hands of Hawkeye, which would perhaps not be the most uplifting thing to hear at the of your life, don't you think?" a man asked, taking Cooper's book in hand. The shelves at the St. Marcouf library were tightly packed and thinly spaced, so Meredith, who was looking at the selection of American history, was forced to brush against the stranger's shoulder as she turned, bringing her ear around in his direction.

"I'm sorry?" she said.

"Nothing, excuse me Ma'am. It's just, this book, *The Last of the Mohicans*, have you read it?"

"No, I haven't," she said. "I'm afraid I don't know so much about literature."

"No harm done." The man picked out two editions of the book from the section on literature in a foreign language. He browsed them both, holding one under his right arm while he inspected the other. Choosing one, he put the other back on the shelf in the wrong location.

The man looked up and saw Meredith watching him make the choice between books, "It is not for me, but rather for a woman I met recently at hospital. Nothing serious. For me. I mean. Just a routine look about. But this woman I met, Mrs Purcell, is dying. Although I can see not much more wrong with her than a bleak view on life, which can be a hindrance but rarely, at least in my experience, an actual cause of death. A couple of days ago I mentioned the Schubert story to her, hoping to put her in a more realistic frame of mind by naming the spirit she felt was haunting her. You know, death. But she just simply asked me to procure the book for her. I've been to this little lending library before, for research, and so here I am again."

"The Schubert story. Is that what you were mentioning to me?"

The man nodded. "I read the novel only last year myself, while doing some research."

"So you are a professor."

"Biographer."

"Well, this woman sounds like quite a handful. I wish you the best of luck."

Meredith left the stranger with his book and made her way to the exit of the lending library. She passed three circular tables with stiff-backed chairs, three to a table. She put her book down on the check-out counter. The librarian turned the book over so she could see the title, looking at Meredith all the while as if to say that an upside-down book was only the beginning. The librarian opened it up to take out the check-out card. It was then that Meredith first realized what she had done. While talking to the man she had absentmindedly taken a book from the shelves, and now here she was at the counter. It was Hansler's *A Brief Outline of the History of the American Locomotive*. Meredith could do little more at this point but admit that she did not speak French and that she did not own a library card.

"Would you like one then?" asked the librarian in English as correct and stiff as the chairs.

"I don't know what is involved in the process."

"A simple proof of residency."

"But I am staying at the Veloped Hotel."

"Does Mrs Pixous know you are trying to take out a book under her name?"

"That is not what I am doing."

"I'm not sure she would see things in such a light."

"Wait," said the man Meredith had met in the stacks, now standing behind her in line. He was the only other patron in the library at the time. The man was holding his book right-side-up with his library card trapped under a thick yellow thumb. "I think I can help," he said.

HENRY'S SECOND INCARCERATION was interrupted by a hanging. It was not his own. He showed up early, as he was told to do. He did not want to do anything untoward to draw any more attention to himself. The woman being hanged had not yet made her appearance, but Henry was able to gather some information from the crowd from which he was standing slightly apart. Her name was Juliana Connolly. She had been put to death, ostensibly, Henry now thought to himself, for repeated thievery and cavorting. However, and this seemed to be the common opinion of a number of gossips in his immediate area, she was actually being punished for another reason. Not that it was for having an affair with Charles II at his country home in the south, nor for bearing him a child, nor for giving the child the King's name. Instead it was thought that Juliana was being hanged for an unreasonable demand: she asked for the child to be clothed in the livery of the court. She could not bear to see her little Charles, aged three, going about like an urchin. It happened that on points of dress Charles II was rather sore at the moment, and not only because of the repeated requests of the Chapel. Demands were coming in from all fronts: new hats for the cooks, aprons for the housemaids, cuffs for the footmen. So in response to Juliana's request to clothe the boy, the King, out of a rage his position did not allow him to regret, sent her to her death as a thief and cavort. Juliana was sentenced to hang until dead. It gave Henry a break from his cell.

He was to clean up after the hanging: to gather the head and haul the body, to wipe the blood and pick the blade clean. There was a loose head after a hanging because after being hanged the head was severed from its neck, just to ensure death. This extra precaution existed because of two cases of hanging survivors in recent memory where, after twenty-four hours of suspension, the sentenced did not die. Upon examination by the court alchemist the two criminals had been released out of fear of divine retribution, since they had somehow survived the rope. All this did was to make Charles II instigate a six-hour hanging and then the hatchet rule, both to forestall any ideas of divine interference and to make sure that the punished were exactly that.

Henry edged his way closer to the gallows, not to get a better look at the convict, for Juliana had not been brought out yet, but to hear two men discussing the apprehension of the "garment-mad" woman. The gist of their conversation ran as follows: they got her and they got her good. When the King's guard burst into her room Juliana was found with the gardener. They had young Charles up on the table and both were pretending to admire him in all his courtly finery, although the young boy was actually dressed in a dish towel.

AFTER HENRY FINISHED his duties in the courtyard he was returned to his cell rather than back to the stage. Although he had not seen the Captain during the whole day, later that evening he received a letter along with a short, fat candle and a wick which was just about long enough to read the letter twice through before the darkness of his cell returned:

Henry,

After seeing what can only be called the absolutely appalling murder of the Connolly woman today I have arrived at the conclusion that what has come to be known amongst you boys as "services," but amongst the clergy and administration as "corrective measures," needs to be radically *transmodified*. To put it in brief: I will have nothing more to do with this cloth-hoarding bastard of a king. I think you, as the first servicing two-timer, will agree. Still, seeing a continuing need for corrective measures, which your intransigencies (note — plural!) require, I mean not to end the "services" altogether but (and here comes the explanation of my admittedly curious coinage — *transmodify*) I will *trans*form our services from cleaning up after murders to the much more humane task of diseased-assisting, meaning that we will help assuage the horrors of the plague down in Excester, my hometown. Or at least you will. As for the second half of my new term, I also intend to *modify* your duties. You will assist the syndic whose duty it is to check the inhabitants' residencies. Hopefully you will survive the danger involved, for I need all of my voices in working order for the Christmas concert. (Yes, I am offering that as an outside terminus to your stay. You have probably forgotten that the holiday season approaches, down in your dark prison!). I guess I cannot expect you to react to this news with joy, or relief, or even with a sense of duty to get the job done. But still I think I can expect something from you yet, dear Henry. Even with all the trouble you bring.

To tell you the whole story, my thinking on the subject began today in the courtyard. When I saw Connolly hanged, and I did watch (I did not, like Orpheus, turn away), I thought not only of her but of her boy, young Charles, and I said to myself (although I cannot promise you that, at times, along with the best of us, I do not borrow my thoughts from the words of our great poets, which, after all, is an honour on both sides), that all of us carry the fruit of death inside us: the child a fruit much smaller than the adult, a greener sort but still planted strong, where it grows and reddens and, if left alone long enough, eventually sours, putrefies, and goes back to the earth, invisible and nutrifying. And I could see, Henry, in the instant that body fell (as you know the death is almost instantaneous, most say it is the shock that does them in, making all that hacking the king is requesting bloody unnecessary, and untidy), the boy's fruit flashed from green to red to black to earth all in one moment. His life was over. And I knew, right then I tell you, that I had to make a choice. No longer to clean up after death but to work to conserve life. That is what you will do, starting Tuesday (today is Saturday, in case you've forgotten).

You may, and rightfully so, be wondering why I am writing you. Why not just dispatch you, without a word? The answer is both simple and it is not. I have tried presenting my case for a change to the "services" to the one I am bound by both duty and heart (my Evelyn, your Mademoiselle Cooke) but, if I may be frank, she has been keeping my company less and less, and when she does appear she keeps herself at such a distance that she either claims no interest in my theories (for example, she cannot see need for both <u>trans</u> and <u>modify</u> in my coinage, see above), or she mocks me by repeating what I say but at a higher pitch, much like a cornet imitating a trumpet — oh do not get me started on that subject! So, as I have in you a captive audience, and seeing in you a kindred, sensitive artistic soul, I am trusting you with these words. This letter. I would also like to take the liberty to inform you that your sartorial wealth has been distributed amongst the other boys, who seem to be enjoying it rightly.

I hope to be able to continue this conversation soon. I now must be off. Choir practice awaits.

Safe journey,

Your Captain Cooke

THE MAN IN QUESTION introduced himself as Mr P. A. Austen, Oxfordshire. He was rather heavy-set with a balding crown sporting a tuft of light blonde weeds attempting to cross over. He had unshaven jowls but a clean shirt and tie, no hat and a trench coat. He did little to protect the book under his arm from the light drizzle falling except to have it half-tucked under his right arm, just as he had done inside the library. Meredith put her history in her bag.

Mr Austen's Vauxhall took them to the hospital in under ten minutes. Mr Austen was well informed of the route. "It's like a botany lesson, with all the branching streets," he said. Meredith agreed out of politeness and was not quite sure how she had been swept up and into Mr Austen's vehicle, except that she knew it was drizzling, and that fact alone could free her from any sort of self-criticism. As long as she did not probe her motivations too deeply, which she often did not.

Mrs Purcell's otherwise unoccupied double-room was slightly damp. A sun-faded pea-green curtain was drawn to hide the rain. Mr Austen sat down next to Mrs Purcell's head, on her right side, and indicated the seat on the other side of the bed with an open, wrinkled palm spread out above the sick woman's chest.

"How nice of you to visit, and to bring a friend!" said Mrs Purcell.

"Good afternoon Ma'am. Yes, I have someone with me this afternoon, I hope you don't mind."

"Mind? My goodness, no."

"This is Miss Meredith Haps-Mills. She has a keen interest in Americana, perhaps almost as much as you."

"Pleased to meet you. That should make for some interesting moments, then."

"Pleased to meet you. He's exaggerating, I'm afraid," said Meredith.

"Nonsense," said Mr Austen, "I found her in the American history section. She's checked out Hansler's book on the locomotive. He was a member of the Church of England," he said, but then seemed to wish he could swallow his words.

"The *Outline* or *Modern Railways*?"

"I'm afraid I'm not really sure," said Meredith.

"The *Outline*," said Mr Austen.

"That's fine, dear," said Mrs Purcell. Turning back to Mr Austen, she asked, "Did you find it?"

"Yes, Ma'am. Eventually."

"Excellent. I would like to hear as much as possible before the coma sets in."

"Oh, dear Mrs Purcell," said Mr Austen.

"Coma?" asked Meredith.

"Well, if you had a coma coming wouldn't you desire to hear, at least once in your life, one of the greatest works of American literature? Did you know Schubert requested it at his death?"

"No, I didn't. Wait, yes, I did. I do. Mr Austen told me in the library."

"Then you are completely up to speed, despite your scanty knowledge of Hansler. Now, which one of you is going to read? We should get a move on. Not much time, isn't that right Mr Austen?"

"Yes, you are right," said Mr Austen, turning a bit red and opening *The Last of the Mohicans* to the beginning. Then he handed it across Mrs Purcell's body to Meredith who, startled at the gesture, took it without comment and started reading before Mrs Purcell's coma-bound gaze.

"Mom?"

"Yes, Henry?"

"May I come in?"

"Of course you may, dear." He did. "Mr Austen, Miss, Miss."

"Haps-Mills."

"This is Henry. Henry Purcell. Henry, say hello."

"Hello everybody."

"Henry Purcell," said Meredith, and smiled, "like the composer. What a great name for such a sweet boy. I was just reading your mother a story, about Indians, in fact about the last of the Mohicans."

"His father named him after the composer. I believe Mr Austen knows more about that than I do," said Mrs Purcell, motioning Henry closer, away from Meredith. "He's even been inspired to begin some biographical sketches on the original Henry Purcell, isn't that right?" Mr Austen looked down at his chest proudly. Mrs Purcell suddenly scowled and then turned toward her son. "Now baby, do you remember what mommy is going to have? What mommy is waiting for?"

"A coma?" said Henry. Meredith gently shut the book on her right index finger.

"And what kind of... Come here," she patted the bed in front of Meredith. Henry came around the bed, hands in his navy-blue cotton shorts, and sat down in between Meredith and his mother, without extracting his hands. "That's nice. And what kind of coma is mommy going to have?"

Henry looked around at Mr Austen and Meredith, as if waiting for them to come up with the answer in his place. The rain came down behind the curtains. With no answer coming from either of the two guests in the room, Henry settled back and said with authority, "We don't know yet mommy, but there are four possibilities."

"There are?" asked an incredulous Mr Austen. Henry looked up as if Mr Austen were an idiot, and raised his eyebrows.

"And they are, Henry?" prompted his mother.

"Um, classic, alert, *carus* and," Henry puckered his lips and clenched his fists inside his pockets. "And, the French one."

"Which one is that now?" asked his mother.

"I'm sorry mother, I can't remember," he said, his eyes widening with honesty.

"That's ok, Henry. Isn't it Mr Austen? Miss Haps-Mills? Yes, it is ok for a boy, now and then, to forget what he's taught. We can't be forcing perfection on them all the time, otherwise they won't grow up to love and cherish the memory of their mommies and daddies, will they?"

"I think that's quite right," said Mr Austen. "Very fair."

"Probably so," said Meredith, thinking of her list, now nearly creased into illegibility but still taken with her everywhere.

Henry ran out of the room with his hands still in his pockets and searched for his friend Martino.

THE TRAP CARRYING HENRY had another six hours to go

before reaching Excester when it passed a carriage, overturned and horseless at the side of the road. The driver stopped and shouted his inquiry of whether any assistance was needed. However, apparently it was not, as the trap rapidly departed amid verbose cursing from the driver, who was shaking his fist in the direction of the accident. Due to the incident being outside Henry's field of vision, he was unable to see what was going on, at least until the trap moved forward, removing a tree from between Henry's field of vision and the carriage. Then he saw, seated on the grass and surrounded by food, Evelyn and William laughing, apparently unharmed. They looked as if they had just been thrown into their picnic by a wild wind.

Henry's trap jolted on and its sole passenger became lost in angry reverie. What were they doing, so open in their affections? And why were they so far from London? Together? The more Henry thought about it, the more he was sure that he knew exactly what those overthrown lovers were saying back there on the grass, word for word. He imagined:

"Oh, pass me some wine, my dear Willie!"

"Of course, my dirty little dove."

"Oh, you have not called me that for, oh, I don't know, *minutes!*"

"Yes, it might help if we had a little wine."

"Wine, yes! I forgot. Now where's a servant when you most need one? Sir, the bottles!"

"Yes," William must be giggling at the farce of pretending a servant was in attendance, "hurry up, man!"

Evelyn, mimicking the pouring of wine, "Now there you go, my warm loaf."

"Warm loaf? Where did you come up with that? Or should I even ask?"

"It must be the wine, because I do not know myself!"

"And servant — I could get used to this, you know — servant could you please bring the Madame and I a blanket?"

"Madame is a terrible name, my dear, but at least *you* can think of a pet name."

"What do you mean, *me*? Whoever could not come up with a name for you, my sunfire, my bottle-nose, my Oriental goddess! Was it the unimaginative footman, perhaps? Or one of your other lowlife admirers?"

"Oh you are so naughty, my knight, come and pierce me."

And of course they laughed, after each and every breath, while Henry headed toward a plague-riddled town under lock and key. The only moment of solace he had was imagining that they were just a bit too giddy before the gallows.

"YOU KNOW, A LONG TIME AGO, in Greece, there was an old woman, no one knew her name or anything, and she had some books she wanted to sell. It's hard to say why she wanted to sell them exactly, but she did. Maybe her husband had died in the Samnite war that was going on, I don't know, but she was left alone and she was old. So, let's just say that she had these books and a need for money, for a lot of money. Because the price she asked for the books was out of this world. What did she need the money for? Who knows? Maybe to marry off one of her daughters, but who would have marriageable daughters at her age? She was old, we know that, but we don't know her name. So she wasn't well known or anything, just an old woman. Some people think she was from the countryside, but we really don't know. Anyway, she had these big fat books she wanted to sell and she needed a lot of money. Now another question you might ask is where did she get these books? That's a good question, too. For she was old, not very well known, and in need of money. So how did she come across some books that might be of value in the first place? One thinks, if one is honest with one's self, which we are, aren't we Henry?, we think she probably stole them. Otherwise the facts don't really add up. But look at the evidence: old woman, asking too much for some books. She's from out of town. Sounds like stealing to me. Or maybe she just 'found' them or something. But when people just 'find' things it usually means that they stole them, or didn't leave them for the person who lost them to come back and find them, which is pretty much the same thing, at least according to Kant, the philosopher Kant, and he should know, because he spent a lot of time thinking about these things. But the point of this story is that she took these books to the King, King Tarquinius Superbus. Yes, that's his real name, Superbus. You can look it up. In fact, I would encourage you to do so, since as a researcher myself I would like to sow the seed of research in others, especially in the young. Ok, ok, so how did this woman from nowhere without even a god-forsaken name get in touch with the King, especially King Superbus? I don't know, Henry. Sometimes, and this is another lesson, you just have to admit that you don't know. But she met the King, somehow, we have it on good authority, at least as much authority as we can claim for classical authors, which, if you get down to it, is probably an ok amount, but don't go crazy over it. It is always easy to pick at someone's faults rather than to concentrate on understanding their strong points. But let's just stick to the story, ok? This old woman took these books to this King and asked for a lot of money for them and he said no. Oh, and there were nine books, did I say that already? No? Well nine. So then, the King said no way, that's way too much money you're asking there, so the old woman took three of the books and she burned them. Poof. I guess there was a fire nearby, and a big one, for if you have ever tried to burn a book, not that I have, but I have tried to burn a lot of paper at once, although I can't remember exactly when at the moment. But say a whole week's worth of newspapers or something. It really takes a lot of shifting and poking to get all the paper to burn. You have to be careful it's not just the edges that burn, leaving the insides intact. Especially not if you are burning a book as a threat. Not that I would recommend it. In fact, I would say don't burn books at all. But she does, this old woman, and they are completely burnt, down to the last page. I guess they waited around a bit for it to happen, or it was such a huge fire there, in the King's hall or whatever, maybe a bonfire or something, that they went up like that, poof! But there were three books that were burned, remember. So it must have been poof poof POOF! Then the old woman asked for the same amount of money as the first time, but now for the six remaining books. The King, I imagine, I mean, this is pure conjecture on my part, looked at her a little strangely and said, well, now it's the same price for six books as it was for nine, so, well, no thanks. You know what happened next, then, don't you? I mean, you can guess. The old woman took three more books and burned those too, probably in the same successful and rapid way that the first three were consumed. It was then that Superbus got all worried, for there were only three left, and the woman didn't even have to ask again for the original price, because the King gave it to her right away. Then he took the three remaining books, put them in a temple, created a council eventually called the *quindecemviri sacris faciundis*, but don't worry about that, it's not really important. Anyway, Superbus created this council to consult the books as if they were oracles from the gods about how to deal with politics and whatnot. I guess they contained some kind of information about Rome. But that's not the point. Because the important question really is, well actually, what kind of lesson do you think you can get out of that, Henry? What can you take away from such a wisdom-filled story?"

"Um..."

"A lesson, I mean, about the *ladies*."

"I'm not really sure..."

"Take your mother and Meredith, for instance. You know what I did? When your mum asked me for that *Last of the Mohicans* book, you know what I did? I told her, oh, it would be so hard to find. I had no idea where I could get a hold of it.

31

Whether the book would be available in English. I said that no one looks at the old classics nowadays, even though I knew it would be at the lending library. It had to be. I know my libraries, and I was pretty sure it wouldn't be checked out, because, well, some of those things I said were true, like that no one reads the classics nowadays. That's another lesson. Always tell as much truth in a lie as you can."

"Yes, Mr Austen."

"And when I brought her the book, after a couple of days of 'scrounging,' well, you should have seen her eyes light up! You think she would have gotten so excited if I had just brought the book straight away? No how! Now she thinks the world of me. And then this Meredith saw the whole business too. She was there at the library and then saw me give it to your mother. And now Meredith has fallen for me too. I'm sure of it. She's fallen for me hard, little man, hard!"

ON A PICNIC two weeks after they met at the local lending library Meredith and Mr Austen lay nearly side-by-side on a yellow and green plaid-print cotton blanket on Callie beach. They were not quite side-by-side because the sleeping body of Henry lay between them, curled up against Meredith's left shoulder. Meredith had her arm around Henry, slowly stroking his cheek, and occasionally brushed up against Mr Austen's hairy arm, exposed by a rolled-up sleeve. It was June 5, 1951. Meredith had packed a large lunch consisting of potato salad with peas, cold pork sandwiches and two bottles of Wuse. Mr Austen had just complimented Meredith on her excellent packing skills, for Meredith kept pulling out item after item which caused Mr Austen, quite out of character, or rather, more in character than Meredith had yet been exposed to, to say, "Holy Shit!" to which Meredith, despite herself and again, perhaps more in character than she had been all summer, laughed. But this was before

Henry had woken up, meaning, before the accident.

The accident might never have happened if Henry had worn the bathing outfit he had wanted to, and not the one that was picked out by his mother. Henry had wanted to wear a pair of green army pants that he had cut just above the knee, so that the two big safari pockets could be filled with stones or coal or magazines or, once, pre-war-era pornography he had found further down the beach, way past Mr Setter's fish-cleaning benches. Henry had wanted to wear these pants with what Martino meanly called his "pirate gear," a blue and white sleeveless shirt and a purple scarf, usually tucked into his back pocket when he left home, but somehow finding its way around his neck by the time he reached the beach. But he was only able to wear this ensemble on the mornings he was lucky enough to leave home relatively unmolested by his mother. On mornings like this one, mornings full of plans and picnic baskets, Mrs Purcell was on the lookout, knowing that Henry would probably go in for some new extravagance, such as tussled hair, an untucked shirt, or a bracelet made of dried seaweed. She would usually find him in the bathroom, looking into a mirror seemingly framed by a large, flattened, bridal-like bouquet of artificial lilac and daisy. What Mrs Purcell made Henry wear instead were his white shorts, usually riding high above the waist, and a white-collared shirt tucked in with a blue belt, which matched his blue shoes, shoes he only wore under the most extreme pressure, a pressure Mrs Purcell felt it was her duty to apply this sunny June day. It was these white shorts that put Henry's life in danger.

During the picnic, Mr Austen leaned slowly across Henry's head to whisper something into Meredith's ear. Meredith, perhaps still somewhat afraid of his new-found coarseness, saw Mr Austen's freshly-shaven jowls rapidly moving in her direction and pursed her lips together in a silent shush, directing Mr Austen's gaze to the sleeping Henry by moving her eyes up and down between Mr Austen and Henry's seemingly inert body. Mr Austen halted his advance and, absorbing the new rules of communication laid out, used his eyes to indicate something down beyond Henry's head. Meredith, just beginning to regret the distance at which she was keeping Mr Austen, followed his gaze and saw Henry's shorts sticking up as if with a little tent-pole. In her confusion she didn't know whether to giggle, cry or scream. It was at this moment that a dark wet stain spread from the top of the pole, more heavily in the direction of Henry's stomach, and a salty taste came into the air. Henry's entire body twitched once and he opened his eyes. Meredith gulped and removed her arm from under Henry's head. Mr Austen, not being fully able to process the fact that their silent communication game was over, was wagging his finger and mouthed "no no no." Meredith stood up, shook Henry, and ordered him to go swim in the sea. Henry, groggy and lacking complete control over his motor skills, obeyed as fast as he could, not wanting to realize what had happened. He took a small rowboat out a few yards, which is what they did to swim, to get away from the weeds and things on the shore.

HENRY'S BOAT FLIPPED OVER and was now a wood vault over his bumped head; he banged the sides of the boat as hard as he could with both fists, which was not very hard, for Henry had no purchase to use in order to get a footing for his punches. Once his arm stopped moving, the natural buoyancy of his body restored him to his natural wading level, which, if he kept calm, which he did do now that his fit was over, was at just about chin-level.

Mr Austen looked at Meredith. Henry's banging had subsided on the lake. "Should we go out and get him?" he asked.

"He should be able to work his way out of there himself, don't you think?" Meredith said, surprising herself. She leaned back on her elbows on the plaid-print blanket. Mr Austen, who was also leaning back, had to look through the space between her legs to see the rowboat. Meredith was wearing a thick purple skirt and a white blouse, tucked in, and a matching purple jacket. She had taken off her shoes as soon as they sat down and was wearing cream stockings. Mr Austen was able to see through her legs because the skirt, being heavy and ample, sagged between her knees. It was through this sag that he was able to see the boat under which Henry sulked.

"Do you think he is a good swimmer?" asked Mr Austen.

"A natural average one, I'd guess."

"Oh, really? Why do you say that?"

Meredith sat up. "I would just imagine that would be what Mrs Purcell would say. According to her he's a natural at everything, and I think she did mention swimming among the everythings, although I am not so sure now."

"So we just have to take her word for it then?"

"I did say average. For, you can see for yourself that he is no Frank Wykoff. And plus, I don't see why not trust his mother? Are you always so mistrustful yourself, Mr Austen?"

"Not always, not always. But it is the job of a scholar to find weakness in one's arguments, including those of one's intimates."

"Yes, I see. Is that why you are so..."

"You can say it. Please."

"I don't know if I can."

"Please do, I beg you. My curiosity is peaked."

"Aloof?" Mr Austen laughed. "That's not the right word for it then," Meredith said, smiling downward into her breasts. "Then, alone?"

Mr Austen frowned and leaned back on his shoulders. "*Je sais bien, mais quand même,*" he whispered. Henry's boat was motionless. "Well," Meredith quickly got up and walked down to the shore. She cupped her lace-trimmed hands to her mouth and shouted out to Henry. Henry swam under the boat, abandoning it as he made his way to the shore. Mr Austen joined Meredith.

"Do I need to whisper?" he whispered.

"Why on Earth?" Meredith whispered back.

"Because of your admirer."

"Oh, please. You think Henry is jealous? It's just because of his, because he is a maturing boy and there are far too few people his age around here. It would have been much better for Mrs Purcell to have taken him to the Pacinel beaches in Vida. It's simply overflowing with young bodies. Escaping reality in the surf."

"But then he would have never met you. And perhaps neither would have I," Mr Austen said, poking Meredith lightly in the ribs.

"Stop it. I'm going to get the poor boy a towel," she said, starting up back to the hotel, yet turning around and blowing Mr Austen a quick kiss. Mr Austen blew one back, then turned around and rolled his eyes. He felt like beating the living shit out of Henry when he got back on shore. But the feeling passed.

HENRY'S WORK SOON CONSUMED any time he had for jealousy. His tasks were far more perilous than Captain Cooke had initially indicated in his letter. The town was under quarantine because of a suspected resurfacing of the black plague, which, because of expanded transportation routes through and around the county of Devonshire, could, like any contagious disease, easily spread throughout the county and perhaps even to others. The outbreak was first feared because of the death of Farmer Peterson out near St. David's church. Despite a century of technical advancement, Peterson had done nothing to improve the Peterson sanitation. He was thought to have been infected by a particularly fierce clump of disease stemming from a stymied pool exacerbated by a fiercely humid June. Between that time and Henry's arrival three other deaths in the town, all downstream from the Peterson farm (now burned), brought down a county-wide quarantine.

The quarantine procedures that were developed during the last bout of plague had nearly been forgotten. But not quite. At least not by the officials. The families of the town were kept to their homes for a period of 21 days, 7 days longer than the known gestation period of the disease. If there was a death in a household at any time during that period a candle was to be held to a window while the syndic made his morning rounds. The body was to be preserved in the household until evening by the use of salts and garlic.

After a death (and many were to follow the original four bodies), the time of quarantine was reset for the household. During this period food was to be passed through a specially constructed "cat door." The door was a small hinged panel at the bottom of the entryway. It was around this cat door that Henry's duties revolved. Captain Cooke's instructions indicated that Henry was to be put to use by Syndic Pinker as registrar of food and drink, which involved the assembly and recording of food pallets at the cook's station, mornings and evenings. What came as a surprise to Henry was that Syndic Pinker altered Cooke's original orders. Pinker was to retain all record-keeping rights and Henry was merely to deliver pallets door-to-door, but only to those houses which had not equipped themselves with the cat door. Pinker retained the privilege of serving cat-door-blessed houses because, having been made familiar with the many ways of earning one's way from a young age (his father, as soon as the quarantine was over, was to be reinstated in the city gaol on debt charges), he found in his newly promoted duty as Syndic the opportunity not only to visit all rank and file of quivering town folk in their households, but, as he controlled the inflow of food and drink from a safe distance, the opportunity to extract any number of post-quarantine favours and promises (provided he survived, which he did). Therefore Henry was given the duty of calling on the cat-doorless houses. This meant the houses of those unable to hire anyone to construct the device. These people were obviously of less interest to Pinker, and, because of the need to fully open the front door of their homes, they were also seen as a greater health risk. Therefore these became the doors on which Henry was to call, and which were to open on an opportunity for Henry to forget all about Evelyn, at least for the time being.

UPON KNOCKING at the last house on Waterbery Street, Henry found a young, seemingly healthy woman behind the door. He gestured toward his self-drawn cart he had set down to rest. "Good day, Mademoiselle. Food and such. Could you let me know how many portions? I mean, how many of you there are?"

"Well, one thing I can tell you for sure is that there are not enough of us. Not enough occupants. Not enough portions needed. But before you pour out your well-meant but idiotic sympathy, what has happened to Syndic Pinker? No harm, I can only imagine."

"No, no harm, no harm. Just a bit of a shake-up. I'm new. And I'm sorry. But I am glad there are still people left to serve in your household, for my knocking at many of your neighbours' doors has gone unanswered, if I may be so bold."

"You may," she said, "but just be aware, there's nothing for your kindness here."

"I do not expect anything, Mademoiselle. Just how many, if you may?"

"Left you with us poor scum, has he? Opening our doors onto the foul stench of death? You can come by again tonight. We've lost Uncle Toby, I might as well tell you, although I fear it's down to starvation more than anything else. So now there are three. Three portions. No more."

"I am sorry, Mademoiselle."

"What a bastard. I mean, not you. Sorry. Him. Pinker. I mean, thank you. I guess."

"It's alright. So, tonight, then," Henry said, picking up the reins of his cart and making his way down the rest of the street of cat-doorless doors.

MRS PURCELL SETTLED BACK in her bed, curtains drawn. Mr Austen was reading to her. They had finished, along with Meredith's help, *The Last of the Mohicans* and were now on *Heart of Darkness*, at Mrs Purcell's request. She had heard that it had been the last book Virginia Woolf had reread before taking her own life.

"Now this is strange," said Mr Austen, creasing a page flat with his plump yellow finger.

"Not again, Mr Austen. Please."

"But the Swede, the Swede. I have come across some interesting notions of a Swede in my research on Purcell the composer. And now, here, in this paragraph, I am just about to read to you, I mean this paragraph here, there's another Swede."

"Yes, well, that's nice. Two Swedes. I think there are many more of them, actually. But please continue reading. It's getting late."

"Yes, but this Swede in the book, and the Swede of my research. Both on the same day. I can't imagine that's too common, now is it?"

"The Swedes have been around for ages, Mr Austen. Surely your research has taught you that much."

"Just one moment, please."

Mrs Purcell pulled up the blankets on her bed a bit closer to her chin while Mr Austen quickly skimmed ahead. The light from the reading lamp on her nightstand was enough to bring the book on Mr Austen's lap out of the shadow, for he held it quite far away from himself due to his far-sightedness, caused as he said from a voracious program of reading he had undertaken in his college days, doing Greats. Mrs Purcell was left in the dark, although in the dim haze of the outer reaches of the lamp one could make out her black curly hair pulled back over her skull by a hairpin, and the neck of her green nightgown pulled up tightly around her chin.

"Ah, yes. Listen to this. I excerpt. Oh, Marlow is speaking, as you know. So, here it is: 'I had my passage on a little sea-going steamer. Her captain was a Swede...' And there's more. Because this Swede mentions another Swede he met there in Africa. Can you imagine that? Three Swedes, one in my research, and here, two in Conrad's book: too amazing to be a coincidence. This deserves a paper! There are so many connections to draw, and who else is there to draw them if not me? So listen, the Swede the first Swede mentions here in the book, he hung himself! He couldn't take it in the jungle. This first Swede says, answering Marlow's question of why he hung himself, he says, wait a second, here it is, 'Who knows? The sun is too much for him, or the country perhaps.' Amazing. And even more, this Swede in my research, he was a viola player, also out of his 'natural' element. Because he was a Swede who moved to England and, after failing at becoming a *famous* viola player, was sort of drafted into minding a prison. And now in Conrad this first Swede, I mean the one in *Heart of Darkness*, are you following me?, was also out of his element, because he was telling his story sitting on a ship on the Thames at the edge of London, where, you will remember, since it was only a few pages ago, Marlow began his journey. And this 17th-century Swede of my research eventually hung himself too, right after the plague kind of died out. He was in London. They were having all of these concerts and things for the King, because it was the end of the plague. But the Swede took his life there. In a newly built orchestra pit, really the first of its kind. No one has ever really figured out why though. Why he hung himself, for he left no note and, because not only of the scandal of suicide, but also because of the location of the deed, it was hushed up, I believe. In fact there is only a passing reference to the event in the book considered one of the main sources of information for that period I am talking about, this book called the *King's Musick*, where it says something like, and I can't quote this for you verbatim or anything, but it is something like 'where the prison guard known only as the Swede was found naught but with an apple in hand and a flush of crimson shame at not fulfilling his musical potential.' An apple! Crimson joy! Potential! Conrad! Oh, there is so much there. What a paper! And to think, no one has come across this before!"

"And then what?" asked Mrs Purcell.

"What do you mean, 'and then what?' I have to flush out the connections, read, investigate, interpret."

"No, that second Swede hangs himself, and then what? In Conrad's story, Mr Austen. That you're here to read, if you please."

"Oh, yes. Well I suppose we should go on then, Mrs Purcell," said Mr Austen, while preparing the book with a bit of a flourish. "Where were we then?"

"AND THEN YOU HAVE A LINE like that. You could base a whole novel on a line like that. A detective novel. You have all the clues right there, or, maybe not all the clues but the solution. That could be the last sentence of a detective novel, all the answers right there."

"Where?" asked Mrs Purcell.

"Around that boy's neck."

"Sorry, I guess I wasn't really listening. I mean, this novel has a lot of description in it, don't you think. I mean, what boy? I thought you were talking about Marlow. Is he a boy? Isn't that kind of young to be captain of a ship or whatever?"

"Not Marlow. The boy. Ok, I'll back up a bit. I guess it's more than one sentence, a couple. But you know what I mean. It's an episode, a detail. *Passim*."

"We'll never get through this thing. I thought you said it was short?"

"So it's like this..."

"But then again, I guess in a state like mine, I should be grateful for anyone willing to uplift my last days even in the slightest."

"'The man seemed young — almost a boy —'"

"What I really should do is thank you, Mr Austen, for your attention. God knows my son is off who-knows-where with who-knows-whom. And me with a coma coming on. Have you met that Martino boy? They always seem to be in some kind of strange trouble together."

Mr Austen raised his voice a little, "'...but you know with them it's hard to tell. I found nothing else to do but to offer him one of my good Swede's ship's biscuits I had in my pocket.' See, here we have the Swede again. Many pages later, suddenly the Swede appears again. I do think I'm onto something here. 'The fingers closed slowly on it and held.'"

"I wouldn't mind a biscuit."

"What?"

"Nothing."

"Sorry?"

"That Swede sure seems to like biscuits."

"But this is the first time the biscuits are mentioned. You have no way to support your argument."

"But think of it Mr Austen. Out there in Africa, so far away from home, and with a nice tin of biscuits. A man must surely love his sweets to make that kind of effort."

"But you have misunderstood the whole point."

"I bet that's the answer to the mystery. The biscuits. It's what you called, when we were reading *The Last of the Mohicans*, an 'incongruent element' if I remember rightly. Something that doesn't fit, that sticks out. So it has to be a clue."

"That's preposterous. *Heart of Darkness* does not have 'clues.'

And who ever heard of a detective novel based on a tin of biscuits? There were countless items of Western European origin in Africa at the time. The explorers practically brought the whole lot of Selfridges with them."

"Just keep your eyes on those biscuits. You'll see."

"Fine. We'll keep our eyes on the biscuits then. But listen up, and I think you'll see my point: 'The fingers closed slowly on it and held — there was no other movement and no other glance. He had tied a bit of white worsted round his neck.' Why? Where did he get the worsted rope? Was it a badge, an ornament, a charm, a propitiatory act? Was there any idea connected with it at all? 'It looked startling round his black neck, this bit of white thread from beyond the seas.'"

"Biscuits," said Mrs Purcell in a giggle. Mr Austen caught the laughter too.

"I think you might be right after all, Mrs Purcell," he said, heading to the hospital kitchen to see what he could round up. "Biscuits. I'll definitely have to take them into consideration."

PINKER WAS BUSY extracting a favour, so Henry had to drag Uncle Toby's body all by himself. He tried not to imagine the gruesome difficulties the family had in bringing Uncle Toby to the door. Henry had to drag Uncle Toby by his feet, climb up onto the empty body cart, and then heave the body on top. The woman he had met earlier that day held the house door open all the while.

Her name was Cathleen and she and Henry broke the rules of quarantine three days later. In fact, Henry and Cathleen broke the rules not only by leaving the confines of Cathleen's house (which was twice forbidden because of the recent death of her uncle, which had reset the quarantine clocks back to zero for the whole family), but also by leaving the street and nearly the town proper. Cathleen knew a place where they could have had a swim if it had been warmer. It seemed like as good of a place as any to go since Henry knew of little more than his three streets, the food station and the new graveyard. But Cathleen knew all the nice spots around town, and her first choice was the swimming pond out near Bonbay Null. It was there she had shared her first kisses with a farmer's son, and she entertained the sad belief that it was perhaps the spot more than herself that was the cause of her first romantic engagement. Even if she did smile at herself for the silliness of the thought, she would rather not upset the stars in any way by bringing Henry to untested ground. Despite the grave situation of the town in general, and her family in particular, Cathleen even started to quietly sing to herself on the way.

Sneaking away from house and street was relatively easy since there was no one about except for Henry and Pinker, and Henry knew Pinker's routine and was able to guide them clear. Henry, upon taking Cathleen's arm once they were out of sight of her home, jokingly called out to the absent Syndic to arrest them both for breaking quarantine, a joke which got him at first a stern look at such disruptive behaviour but then not only a squeeze from the crook of Cathleen's arm, but direct and warm eye contact as well.

"This is it," she said, as they came out of a thicket of oak trees to a rather small but clean pond hidden both from the road and from the Bridewell. "It's small but private, a place where I must admit I have visited previously, but, I also must tell you with what you might perceive as a sparkle in my eye, I am also privy to the fact that this place contains the charm of fairies, at least as far as two newly christened lovers are concerned."

"You work fast," said Henry.

"There's a plague," said Cathleen.

"Oh, really?" said Henry, immediately regretting his tone as Cathleen, pretending not to notice, and seemingly not giving a care for the pale-green dress she had on, sat down on the ground just beneath her. Because of the unexpected hardness of a stone covered in moss, this quick movement squeezed a very feminine "Humph" from the top of her throat. She smiled into her bosom.

"Sorry," said Henry. "It's just that..."

"It's just that you spend your days feeding people who might make you sick just by their sight? That you spend your nights carting away the dead, realizing that you will have to touch them, your healthy skin against their sick, so that there is nothing for you to do but muster a kind of bravado so that if you do not make it through this trial, and it is a temporary trial for you Henry, I know it is, then you will be remembered as brave, and if you can't muster the courage, you will at least be remembered as kind, or at worst foolish, maybe even reckless, which is pretty close to brave? You might just as well be a knight. Anyway all that is better than being cowardly, which you are not, let me tell you."

"You might be right," Henry smiled.

"So this bravado must invariably lead to a kind of uncouthness. Which, I must say, is not particularly attractive. Although much the same goes on in all the homes of this town, including my own. However, being uncouth might not be the best path to follow if you are at the side of a secluded lake to which a young woman has brought you. If that happens to be the case, then I would recommend that you change your tactic, so that you do not lose sight of the lovely wench before your cups are filled."

"I would indeed be foolish to throw away such freely given advice. In fact, Cathleen, may I call you Cathleen?"

"You may."

Henry sighed. "Then Cathleen, what I would like to do is to take your advice."

"So be it," she said, "now you just listen to me, and take my hand," which Henry did.

"I REALLY THINK you should go with her. I mean really go with her, she sounds perfect for you, Henry. Just your type. And she sings for you? Good God! What else do you want? You know that a woman who sings for you will do just about anything, you know what I mean? All those things you can't even talk to that Martino friend of yours about.

"I really think you should go after her. After quarantine I mean, of course. Assuming she makes it and all. And I'm sure she will, for your sake. Even considering the rest of the family's dropping like flies. You said you carted away poor old Toby? It might just be her and her half-wit brother left then. Maybe a distant cousin. But she seems to be doing alright. Probably eats a lot. How much are you giving her anyway? Started sneaking her extra portions yet? If not, you should. I mean, it's love, so don't hold back.

"And then for the wedding I think you should keep it small. Just friends and family. And she should wear white. She's been engaged before, you know. Yes, to a farmer's boy. He sung too, but not in the choir, like you. In the shop he apprenticed at. The butcher's. He had as little to do with his land as he could. Went up to London and wasn't expected to come back to his business. In meat I mean. But he did come back. Never told anyone why. He came back and worked for his butcher but seemed to have lost interest. Would sing in his office above the shop, though. That's how they met. She heard him and stopped outside to listen. Then joined him she did, at least that's how they told it. Then he died two months before you arrived. Can only whistle to the worms now.

"She must be pretty enough for you too, I think. Pretty enough for just about anyone from these parts. And with that nose of yours you can't really be all that picky, now can you?"

"Yes, but..." Henry was cut off by a knock at the door. They were in the food pallet storage shed, just inside Bear's Gate, which was the main entrance to the town. It was a knock which turned into Evelyn entering with a minimum of entourage.

Dismissing an introduction to Pinker, Evelyn took Henry aside and semi-officiously whispered in his ear: "I come here on the express will of Captain Cooke himself, to check on your moral improvement. I hear you have gotten to know the local customs quite intimately."

"Evelyn, what a load of crock," said Henry. He was thinking of Cathleen, William and the others. Pinker started at the familiar address.

Evelyn smiled briefly and led Henry out of the shed with a firm hand. Pinker tried to make eye contact with her entourage as they turned around to leave but he did not stand a chance.

"LISTEN, A WHOLE WORLD is tied up in that sentence. A whole mystery, the solution to a problem. It could be the last sentence of a detective novel," Mr Austen said. He was sitting with Henry on the stairs outside the hospital, waiting for Mrs Purcell to come out. "Your mother doesn't understand a thing." Henry played with the sole of his sandal that was beginning to peel away, aggravating it further. "Listen to this, I have it right here," he said, taking the book out of his back pocket. There was now a thick crease in the spine, along page 67. "'He had tied a bit of white worsted round his neck', can you believe it? An African, way out there in the jungle, having this piece around his neck. Do you know what worsted means? Worsted: closely twisted yarn, very thin. You might not know that word. It's pretty advanced."

"I know 'worsted'. I'm not stupid, you know."

"Yes son, but please don't feel the need to lie just now. It's ok not to know everything. That's something a man has to come to grips with at some point in his life, you know. That he doesn't know everything. Because he looks like a fool lying."

"But I know 'worsted'."

"And how do you know it, pray tell?"

"I know lots of things you think I don't: Like the capital of Spain and where the first summer Olympics were held, and I know the country where Joseph Conrad was born. Lots. Mom says you over-teach."

"Over-teach? That sounds pretty dramatic now, doesn't it? Now what do you think this word, 'over-teach' means?"

"That you tell people things they already know. Then they think you're foolish because of it."

"I see. Did your mother provide you with that definition or did it come out of your sweet, curly, blonde mop all by itself?" Mr Austen took a breath, wiped the sweat from the back of his neck and said, "Ok then, you seem to know just about everything there is to know. So what do you know about this?" He took out a postcard that was wedged between the last page and the back cover of the book.

Henry took the postcard with both hands, as if it were made of tissue paper. As if he knew what was on it already. It was a black-and-white photo. It looked like from before the turn of the century. It was of a woman riding a horse. But the woman was naked, and the horse had no saddle. And the woman was leaning forward, or, as Henry saw as he examined the postcard more closely, she was pulling herself forward by holding on tightly to the horse's mane. Her hair was parted in the middle, blonde, and curly. Some strands from the right side of her part came over her front shoulder but did not block the viewer from seeing her breasts. The left part presumably tumbled down her back. The woman was looking out from between the part in her hair, which separated just above her eyes. She was looking right into the camera. The horse pointed toward the edge of the frame.

"What do you know about that?" Mr Austen asked again. The postcard was becoming damp under Henry's taut fingers. "Or, maybe a more accurate question, one that could tease out some more juicy information than a simple sardonic 'nothing,' would be *what do you think she is doing*?"

Henry did not look up from the postcard. Mrs Purcell came out of the hospital and up to the set of stairs where Henry and Mr Austen sat. She stood behind Mr Austen, who was sitting on the top step going down from the entrance. Henry was on the bottom step. She could not see the postcard because Henry had stuck it into his shirt pocket. Then Meredith came up from the direction of the beach, wrapped tightly in a towel that was pulled up to her neck, thus exposing her upper thighs. She saw the postcard right away, showing through the thin fabric of Henry's shirt, although what was on it was not clear. She jokingly tugged it out, looked at it, dropped it to the ground, and thought of slapping Henry's right cheek. Mrs Purcell stood up, slowly walked down the steps while staring at the distressed look on Meredith's face. She picked up the postcard, looked at Henry, and then at Mr Austen. Mrs Purcell returned the postcard to its rightful owner amidst a number of protestations about research. This was a few weeks before Mr Austen was found murdered on the beach.

Part Two

HENRY'S FIRST PUNCH landed square on William's left eye, scrunching the pupil and bruising the cheek. Then he pushed William back with his chest, deep into the backstage curtains, dark purple and made especially for the theatre by M. Chandelle, from Reims. In short, Henry bashed the lights out of William. This was on his first night back in London, just hours after his arrival, since Evelyn took Henry straight to the Chapel upon getting into town. The fight took place backstage, right before stepping out for the first practice for the Christmas concert. This concert was the reason Henry had been brought back from Excester, and William had been made first chair cornet when Henry left. Upon first seeing Henry, William offered a warm welcome home, as did the few other boys who were around. It was the warmth of the welcome that unhinged Henry. If he had been greeted coldly, competitively, or not at all, he could have managed. But, upon being received as a friend, as second chair in fact, Henry was unable to control his temper and lashed out. As the fight played on the interest of the boys turned to the stage curtain parting. The most eager of the choirboys decided to slip through, more interested in catching the Captain's attention than watching a scrap. They were dying to get into the first and most visible row of the choir on the first day of practice, when the Captain assigned the places for the concert. Plus they wanted to get away from the fight in case anyone was to be sent to the now more extensive "service." Henry obviously did not give a damn as he continued whacking William. Most of the other boys made their way on stage.

Martino got between Henry and William. He had put himself there purposefully to avoid elongating what he thought had been a prolonged absence of his best friend, whom he was now seeing for the first time since his return.

"Let's take it easy now, Henry. I don't care what is going on between you and William, but I don't want to see you back in the green room again, alright?" said Martino, holding back William's attempt at repartee.

"Go to hell, you idiot!" screamed Henry, "The both of you!"

BESIDES WILLIAM'S PROMOTION, Henry was worried because Cathleen had promised to come up to London for the Christmas concert to see him. Syndic Pinker was supposed to bring her. There was no telling what would happen when she entered his choir-boy world. She had no idea about Evelyn, although Evelyn knew all about her even before she arrived in the country. It did not bother Evelyn one bit, and she encouraged the continuation of the country romance while he prepared to return to the city. Now there were two weeks left before the concert, and hence Cathleen's impending arrival. Henry was afraid that Evelyn was not really as calm about everything as she seemed. She had more than enough time to plan what she would do when Cathleen showed up.

EVELYN AND CATHLEEN first met outside of Evelyn's chambers. Cathleen had been asking the Captain about how best to reach Henry amid the cavernous halls that made up the Chapel. Evelyn had been in the chambers at the time, but exited a back way, only to circle around and meet up with Cathleen as she exited Evelyn's own apartments.

"It's you," said Evelyn.

"I have a name, you know. It's Cathleen, Cathleen Numm."

"Then I shall call you... the Hussy. How does that sound to you? Your own personal big-city nickname. The Hussy."

"I would prefer Miss Numm, or Cathleen if you must, or

Cathy like my Uncle Toby called me. Actually, no. That wouldn't be acceptable, just Miss Numm, please."

"And why has Miss Numm travelled so far to grace our small choir with her presence? Perhaps she has her eyes on a man, and which one might that be? Someone in the choir, since you were behind my husband's door? Unless it is him that you seek. In that case, you may have him. However, maybe it is someone else? If it is a man, I have probably had some dealings with him. And there is quite a list. Let us see, is it Ralph? No, Jasper? He's left for the country. Maybe someone a bit closer to the choir... William? I do not have much interest in him any longer... Or maybe it is Henry, Henry Purcell, son of Thomas and our pride and joy. Henry who went off to Excester in your disgusting little Devonshire and came back with a thing he calls a 'music piece' about a lovely wench he insists is me, but who is just too sweet for me to believe it. However, the Captain has ordered the 'piece' to be performed and there is little I can do except set the stage on fire. And I do mean that literally, as an actual possibility. But that just would not do, for someone could get hurt, not you I mean, but Henry, or Ralph. Ralph has such a weak complexion, I do not know how he would survive a fire and still be fit for the sheets."

"You really can't be that awful," said Cathleen.

"Just for you my dear."

"Well, we'll let Henry decide then."

"Let Henry decide what, exactly?"

"Well, decide."

"Why in heaven would he be the one to decide?" asked Evelyn. "And do you not have anything more intelligent to talk to me about besides a man? There are worlds of things to discuss, and yet we spend our time talking about him, Henry. We could even be friends, not enemies. But alright, dear. I shall call him right in. He will be right here, my Cathy, in front of us both in a moment. And then we will see what the little beast does."

"I'LL DO IT," said Meredith, "I think he would have wanted me to. He, well, dropped some not-so-subtle hints really on more than a number of occasions. Yes, I could say that he wanted me to do it. I mean, if it ever came to this, which it has. I mean, now that he's gone. There are things to think of, aren't there? All this can't just go to waste. There are so many, papers, you know. So many things."

"Think of all that effort," said Henry.

"Yes, the effort," said Martino. "Very good point, Henry. Meredith. Glad to see you're both keeping your heads together in all this. I mean, a man was just killed, on the beach, and Meredith, you're thinking of his papers? You want to write a biography of a biographer? Is that it? Do you think you're funny or something?"

"No, Martino," said Meredith. "It's just that, well, he gave me a number of hints that if anything were to stop him from completing his work, he would want me, to help."

"She's just making a kind gesture, Martino," said Henry. "Relax a little."

"Ah, yes," said Martino, putting his hands in his pockets, and acting very adult all of a sudden. "The *beau geste*. I wonder where that will lead you? Fame and fortune at the cost of a murder, maybe? Detached house, butlers and servants when this whole mess is over?"

Meredith looked up from the open suitcase of letters sitting on Mr Austen's neatly made bed. One of her legs was tucked under the other. "Not so likely, Martino," she said. "Fame and fortune? You think that's what Mr Austen is about? Well I don't think so. And Martino, you have no right to be so flippant after a murder. It's ghastly."

"Mother said she saw some of his books in a shop once," said Henry, "In London."

"*Mother said she saw some of his books in a shop once,*" mimicked Martino. "In *London*."

"Well, I have to respect the man's wishes," said Meredith. "And I think that ends the discussion right there."

"What exactly were these wishes, then?" asked Martino. "Have anything in writing?"

"Martino!" said Henry.

Meredith untucked her leg, put both feet on the floor, firmly, stood up and started putting the papers she had spread around the bed back into Mr Austen's suitcase, as if she were afraid someone would steal them. "He asked me, once, when his eyes got tired, if I could take his dictation."

"And...?" asked Martino.

"Well, I did," said Meredith.

"And that's it?" asked Martino.

"Really, what else do you want?" Henry asked his shoes.

"What else? Where to start? Dictation? Did he think he was bloody Milton? He asked you to do dictation and now you think you own all his, papers and things? Sorry, but I don't quite follow."

"You're just sore because you want the postcards," said Henry.

"And leave Milton out of this," said Meredith.

Martino looked up at Henry, stared at him hard and stormed out of the room. Meredith shut the neatly packed suitcase. "Henry," she said, and patted the back of his hand. Henry whimpered. Meredith picked up the suitcase and said, "I'm sorry, Henry. I shouldn't be treating Mr Austen's things this way. Martino does have a point. But you know, Mr Austen had so many good ideas, it would be such a shame to let them alone. And then, two nights ago, Monday, how long and how short ago that was! Mr Austen mentioned something else to me, that he had found a manuscript, one that everyone thought had been burned, an old one, and that he was preparing it for publication. He said he had it with him, here. I couldn't find it. But you know, it should be here, somewhere. And it should see the light, don't you think Henry? It should see the light." At that Meredith left the room with the suitcase tucked under her left arm, just as Mr Austen had done with *The Last of the Mohicans* in the lending library back when he was alive.

HENRY NEVER CAME. Cathleen eventually grew bored and went to find him on her own. No one would give her any information and eventually, after weeks of asking, her money and patience and affection started to wane and everyone who thought about her assumed she had already gone back home. Henry was being held prisoner, naked, confined in bed, with the door locked. Evelyn kept the room cold and his body well fed. Evelyn would make Henry practice, repeatedly until he got it right, right meaning slower. And he had to do it over and over again because he was becoming so exhausted, while at the same time in a hurry to complete his performance. Therefore it would often take many tries to get it right.

A list of things Henry would do during the moments Evelyn was out of the room could include:

Try to keep his eyes open long enough to decide whether it was night or day.

Turn the sheets inside out. They were white on both sides. He wanted to see if Evelyn would notice. She would, every time.

Try on Evelyn's clothes that she would leave behind. She never caught him at this.

Bathe in the facilities in the NW corner, under the straw-stuffed window.

Unstuff the straw from the lower left-hand corner of the shuttered window and look out at the meadow fading into the wave of oak on the Stratton, and then try to see beyond that group of trees by squinting but he was unable to see much more.

Take a knife that had once fallen from a breakfast tray and continue carving a story he had started into the underside of the bed frame that, so far, ran: "At the edge of the greatest forest in Eng."

Try to peek into different places of his body Evelyn had recently explored. This was done mainly by lifting both of his ankles behind his neck and rolling as far as possible onto his back.

Try to hide in different places in the room so that when Evelyn came in she would think he had been captured (except for the fact that the door was locked — no matter how hard Henry tried, which was not that hard, really, to open it, he was frustrated, even when employing the story knife). Henry was only able to successfully do this twice, since he usually had to wait in his place for so long that he became cramped or bored or tired and he would leave before her arrival. On the two times he had stayed she found him straight away.

Pray to his God that He would allow Captain Cooke to die, perhaps by contracting the plague, which would then force the rest of the house into quarantine, and for which Evelyn, despite her deepest wishes, would probably have to be separated from Henry, for she could not go missing for that amount of time within her own household (that is for three weeks, minimum, with no deaths) without rousing suspicion. Henry figured that if he survived those three weeks, which he doubted, although his previous confinement in the red and green rooms did boost his chances, he and Cathleen would marry.

Compose *Sinfonia* and *I Was Glad* in his head, eventually writing them down upon his escape, in scarcely altered form.

Fold Evelyn's clothes, neatly, on a chair.

Wrap himself as tightly as possible in the sheets on the floor, hoping to squeeze out his last breath. He came close but never quite made it.

Relive the triumph of the Christmas choir pageant.

Hold his urine for as long as possible since he would have to wait for his waste to be removed, which it was immediately and with much scolding as soon as Evelyn arrived. This would often entail quite elaborate means to keep his mind off his bladder, such as, for example, counting things, like wrinkles on his right index finger, which, from base to nail contained 6 up to the second knuckle, 24 up to the third, 12 up to the cuticle. Another example of deterrence could be imagining the life of Evelyn and whomever she slept with before Henry in this room (he did not know whom, but suspected), what they did together, how often, how loud and how many times. Evelyn had made no secret that she had had others, in order to cure him of what she called his jealousy, something no 17th-century man could afford, for they were past all that now, being modern, educated, and free. Henry eventually agreed. However, it did not work and he was jealous.

MR AUSTEN'S SISTER LUCY came for the funeral, and then arranged to meet Meredith before heading back to London.

Lucy's arrival was announced by the rattle of the sporty AC that brought her. Meredith opened the car door for her. Lucy's body was wrapped in two layers of foulard and on top of that was a fur coat, but faux, for Lucy was a vegetarian, the fact of which had earned her much mocking until it was found that the reason was her health. Lucy was allergic to a number of animal products, including their flesh, skin and milk. Thus Lucy stepped out of the car. Meredith clasped her hands behind her back.

"I am a bit early, I hope you do not mind," said Lucy, extending a hand.

"Not at all. You must be Miss Austen-Baker," said Meredith, kissing a cheek.

They turned toward Meredith's one-bedroom home she had

taken on. "This place, it is lovely. Is that your living room?" asked Lucy, pointing to a window to the right of the main door, a lightly curtained window unsuccessfully hiding a hideous free-standing lamp.

"Beg your pardon?" said Meredith, bringing her fingers up to her exposed throat, a gesture she had never done before.

"Your living room. Paul always sent the most wonderful letters. He was quite the man with words, you know. It was his trade. And he did not spare any on us. Words. He told us all about his dear Meredith's living room. The orange-cinnamon tea. The spiral rug and the green footstool."

"Well, I'm afraid you'll be a bit disappointed. That was at St Marcouf where I first met your brother. I've had to move here since then. The tea does remain an option, however," she Meredith, smiling. Then she opened the door behind her and walked backwards into her own house.

"Lovely," said Lucy, "then we might sit down and I can tell you all about who killed Paul."

MARTINO WAS IN THE KITCHEN drying a serving tray before loading it with biscuits and cheese. He had acquired the cheese especially for Lucy's visit. Meredith and Lucy were in the living room looking at each other.

Martino spent one afternoon a week at Meredith's doing odd jobs around the house. He would trim the grass, water the flower beds, and, with ever-increasing frequency, do general cleaning, which was very light. Martino started cleaning without any special instruction from Meredith. In fact, at first Martino did the cleaning in secret.

It started soon after he had begun helping Meredith out at home. Despite their differences, Martino started spending a lot of time at Meredith's after the death of Mr Austen. This was helped by Meredith and Martino finding themselves lunching together quite frequently at the Purcells', since they had all been thrown together by the tragedy. Martino's cleaning followed the first time he had dared to look in Mr Austen's suitcase, the location of which he had found his first day at Meredith's, now hidden under a new bed. The Victorian postcards were right on top, the ones everyone had seen but him. It was after seeing the postcards that Martino started to clean. Not to clean himself after seeing the dirty cards, and not a cleansing of the sadness of Mr Austen's death, something Martino hardly thought about at all, but rather the postcards released a feeling in him that he could only continue by cleaning, a feeling of warmth and excitement. Like drinking two cups of coffee in a row on the beach, the act of cleaning allowed him to keep this feeling strong. Each motion of his hand holding the dust cloth, a cloth he started bringing himself so that he did not run the risk of Meredith noticing he was using hers, seemed to capture a bit of the feeling of the postcard. For he had a favorite, one that outshone the others. It was the woman on the horse.

Meredith walked in on Martino polishing the mirror frame in her bedroom. Martino liked to clean the things as near to the suitcase as possible. By this time, maybe the sixth time Martino had clandestinely cleaned, he no longer really needed to look at the postcard at all; he could capture the feeling of the card in the act of cleaning itself. Meredith was usually outside, puttering about in the tiny front lawn. Martino found that he had ample time for his activities. She thought he was just preparing lunch. Meredith was out for a long time. She seemed to want to do as good a job as possible weeding the flower beds, a task she usually started before Martino's arrival and finished after he left. But this time Meredith had come into her bedroom, looking for a straw hat to protect her from the sun.

"Martino, what are you doing out of the kitchen?" she said, expecting the worst.

Martino sighed. The feeling was gone. "Cleaning," he said in anger. Meredith laughed.

"I think you have misunderstood my instructions," she said. "I don't think I wanted you to have much to do in here," she said, "in my bedroom." Martino looked at the mirror frame. "Hand me your cloth, please," she said. Martino automatically handed it over. Meredith inspected it, and found it was not a piece of her undergarments. The dust rag was an old male-t-shirt. Nothing of hers. She gave it back, relieved.

"I'll go now," Martino said, and slid past Meredith. He walked straight out of her house and down the block, two houses to his own, not to return until the next week, which he did after Meredith had mentioned her needing his snack-tray expertise. She had asked this in front of Martino and his mother at the grocer's, so that Martino was sure to say yes, which he did. When he nervously arrived he found a whole array of cleaning products on the dining-room table, a larger assortment than Martino knew what to do with. Upon inspection he found he preferred the cloths Meredith had provided to his own. Hers were old handkerchiefs, with embroidered initials that he could not make out, and they were thick and decent. Martino found that they did not absorb the cleaning liquids too quickly, nor did they let them completely run off. He soon found himself coming more often, especially when Meredith had guests, other women from town. She asked him to prepare finger food, which he gladly did, for preparing food meant washing up, and washing up meant finding that feeling.

LUCY, just getting comfortable on Meredith's couch, stopped fiddling with her necklace.

"You said he had a daughter?" asked Meredith.

"Two. Although one died at the age of two months. But this one, the second, lived to be about 13."

"That's horrible."

"Horrible, yes. A good word, 'horrible'. After her death, *The Times* ran a leader demanding an inquest into the circumstances. Some say it was all a miracle, but most a crime. See, one unusually cold autumn evening, Sarah had been taken ill. Her main symptom was vomiting blood. She remained bedridden until her death."

"But I don't see…"

"Paul asserted at the inquest that Sarah had refused all food and drink immediately after her confinement. They were excommunicated from the Church of England, did you know? The whole family became more and more devout as time wore on. Sarah only allowed her parents to apply some water to her lips every fortnight. Said it was 'the tears of Christ' she was tasting. Rubbish. It was all Paul's doing. That's what I say. Sarah was eventually examined by a Dr Fowler, who found her looking very 'spirited' and she had been dressed by her parents as a bride of Christ, surrounded by flowers. *The Times* quoted the doctor as saying something like, 'she appeared to me as a young girl abandoned at the altar and frozen just before shame set in.' Again, rubbish. What need has a doctor for romanticism? He brought a couple of nurses with him (they were later found to be second cousins and not trained for the job in the least) whom he left with the family. No one was allowed to visit, not even me. These nurses were there to make sure the doctor's orders were followed to the letter, and the doctor's orders were to make sure that *no* food passed between Sarah's lips. What a fuck-up. Well, she died. Her faith grew stronger and then she died. Paul was a mix of despair and faith. One rather amazing aspect of the whole thing is that it supposedly lasted two years, from her first confinement to her death. Two years of taking no food, only a little water from time to time. Although one can only assume Paul and his wife were not as strict as all that. You can see why *The Times* said that if she had been born in France or Spain her act would have been declared a miracle. I think it was a miracle Paul was not lynched on the spot. The neighbours caused a riot. Can you imagine, not letting your own flesh and blood eat for two years? What does that even mean? And do you know what he said to me when I asked him? He said: *Je sais bien, mais quand même...* The bastard spoke French to me! Although I am not sure he knew much more than that. 'I know well, but all the same...' What an idiot! Well, Dr Fowler and the nurses were reprimanded, and if you can call a £50 fine anything more than a reprimand then please let me know. But formal charges were brought against Paul, who, coward as he was, upped and moved north, reinvented himself as a travelling scholar, leaving Martha, his wife, alone to deal with the charges, charges that were not to be pressed without the head of house being present, and what a head he was!"

Lucy was interrupted by Martino's entering the room with a tray of cucumber sandwiches.

"My God!" said Lucy, "Is that a *young man*, wearing an *apron*?"

"He helps around the house," said Meredith, smoothing her skirt. Martino set the tray down. "Tea will be right out," said Meredith, "won't it?" Martino winced slightly. Meredith had learned where his buttons lay since discovering his penchant for cleaning. At least she thought so. Lucy cut Meredith's smile short.

"So, no one knows who Paul's killer was, but I'd guess, and this is what I came here today to tell you, that it was an old neighbour. They were all quite upset by the whole ordeal. Or perhaps it was even Martha, his wife. Tracked him down eventually. They argued, and then, confronted with such a beast, what else could you do? Paul was a bastard."

Meredith sat speechless. Martino was frozen in the door frame.

Lucy let out a light giggle, pleased with the response her story received. "It doesn't matter now, anyway," she said, turning quiet and shifting her body back to the sandwiches, indicating the absence of tea with a refusal to put any food on her plate.

BY THE TIME of the Christmas concert there was such a fuss over Henry's absence that Evelyn had to release him from confinement. The fuss was due to the excitement surrounding Henry's debut as both composer and organist. And because of his new ability to grow a moustache. He had made his role in most of the performance rather minimal so that his solo during the final scene would lose no import. What Henry did not expect, once he had the chance to look about him, was to find Evelyn sitting right in front of him, occupying the chair usually reserved for the second of two houtbois chairs.

"What are you doing here?" Henry leaned in and over to whisper.

"Did you not know I play?" Evelyn answered.

"Did I not know you play?"

"An instrument. The hautbois. I thought you knew about music. My uncle was quite an accomplished player at the cloister. But, as the poet says, he was a flower blooming in the desert."

"He was a what?"

"A player. I really can play. I'll show you right now," she said, wetting the reed.

"Are you insane?" Henry asked, leaning in even more and pulling the hautbois down out of her mouth. "You'll get us both killed."

"I didn't think anyone would notice. The text my husband wrote is really so barbaric, I assumed it would just steal the show."

"You read the libretto? I couldn't even make it through it all, and I composed the music for it. I quote," Henry said, rustling a pretend score. Then he glanced up out of the orchestra box and, seeing no one observing him, said "'His absence was Autumn, his presence is Spring / That ever new life and new pleasure does bring / Then all that have voices, let 'em cheerfully sing / And those that have none may rise: 'God save the King!'" Henry put the sheet down. "What rubbish."

Evelyn put the instrument down and walked off the stage. "Well, his rubbish will make you famous," she said.

"HE'S LEAVING!"

"What?"

"I said, *he's leaving!*"

"I heard you the first time, Martino."

Meredith sat down on a floral-print love seat below a window looking onto the main road, which was dusted with dry leaves waiting to catch fire.

Martino continued dusting the picture frames on the wall, starting from the top of each frame, just at the end of feather-duster reach, and worked his way down.

"Now, please, who's going where?" asked Meredith, holding an about-to-be-lit cigarette in front of her mouth while speaking.

"Henry, to America, to look for his father."

Meredith looked up at Martino. Then she looked down at the cigarette, lit it, and looked back up. "His father?"

"He said he worked on the atom bomb. He said he wants to meet him and work with him. To do some research, he said."

Meredith stood up and turned away from Martino. "He's leaving us for the bomb? If he is really making the trip, then he'll have to go to Nevada."

Martino stopped dusting. "Nevada?"

"Or Utah. The radio at the Purcells. It's always talking about such things. That is where they have all the big facilities. The USA. It's quite a long journey. He'll need to bring plenty of underwear."

"Nevada," repeated Martino. "Utah. That's pretty far away. I think Henry was thinking about going back to London or somewhere near there."

"I'm pretty sure it was Nevada," said Meredith, lighting her cigarette. "Or Utah. I'll ask around."

MEREDITH WENT TO HER BEDROOM, pulled the suitcase out from under her bed, opened it up and shook all its contents out onto the floor. If Henry is going somewhere, Meredith thought, then he'll need a properly packed suitcase. Spread across the floor was a barely started biography of composer Henry Purcell, fragments of unfinished poems, and lots of other papers. Papers slipped under the bed, as if too scared to be out. Papers floated softly and landed on Meredith's bright-yellow open-toed slippers. Papers got stuck in the hinges of the suitcase, refusing to leave unripped. Meredith sighed at the mess. And then there were the postcards. A whole stack, spread out. The first visible card was the one of the woman on the horse. It was then that Meredith realized that when she thought of the postcard she had caught Henry holding she only imagined the horse, no rider. The next card was of two women, one on top of the other, one in black heels and the other in white. You could only make out one of the faces, that of the woman on bottom. She was swooning. Meredith put the two postcards back in the stack and straightened them so all their corners were even. Then she put them in her lower right drawer, under some sweaters.

Meredith set the suitcase back on top of her bed and took out the rest of the papers, setting them as neatly as possible on the mess on the floor, knowing she would take care of it all later. She took a pack of cigarettes out of her floral-print bathrobe and lit one using a book of matches from the dresser. She took a shallow drag and put her arms to her hips. Then she put the cigarette out and started to fill the suitcase with clothes for Henry. Most of the clothes were simply the smallest and most boyish things she owned, but the others she bought on her few trips into town.

The first items she packed were two pairs of white cotton shorts. She remembered the time at the lake with Mr Austen. As she folded the four pairs she wondered about how her life would have been different if Henry had controlled himself better that afternoon, and if she had not got so close to Mr Austen. Then she packed an apron, which was white, and was one of the items Martino used when he came over. Meredith sprayed it with a touch of her perfume, and then looked around to check if anyone had seen her. All of the clothes were packed very well. Meredith knew that not only was packing important when traveling, but there was also maintaining one's wardrobe once one arrived. So she put, on the top of all the piles in the suitcase, one slightly chipped wooden hanger.

Then she started gathering the stray papers on the floor, on and under the bed and under the dresser. She put them all in a single pile. She did not worry about face-up or face-down, right-side-up or upside-down, age of paper or color of pen, typed or printed, English or Latin, holy or profane. That kind of organization would come later, and Meredith could hardly wait.

"HE'S NOT GOING ANYWHERE," Mrs Purcell said. "Now please, have some tea." She released her hands from holding the counter top behind her back, pulled out a chair at the kitchen table, and sat down, giving Meredith a wink as she did so. Meredith sat. "Utah, it's just too far away. And his father, what he has done in the war, maybe it was humane in some twisted sense, but to me it was just dishonorable, so let's just leave it at that."

"Are you sure it's not Nevada? I believe the bomb was being worked on in Nevada."

"I don't care if it is happening in France, he's not going."

"There is uranium mining in France, actually," said Meredith. "They have opened up a new mine in a small town called Eles. It was on your radio last weekend."

"Don't insult me," said Mrs Purcell, taking some sugar, "You and the late Mr Austen have done all you can to turn my Henry away from me with your books and such."

Meredith took some sugar too. Then she heard a sound, a kind of slow moaning. As soon as it reached her consciousness she realized she had been hearing it ever since she had sat down. She quickly stirred her tea and put the spoon down on her saucer and took a tiny sip. "It's destiny. You can't do anything about it, Mrs Purcell. I'm sorry. I packed a suitcase for him last night, just so he's prepared, since I didn't think you would be able to face the facts of his leaving."

"Do you hear him moaning?" asked Mrs Purcell. Meredith nodded. "He is in pain because of your encouragement. He wants to go to America, to find his father. Do you understand how embarrassing that is? His father, that lout? Why is this happening to me? So near the end of my days?"

"I beg your pardon?"

"And that boy, Martino. What has become of him?"

"I've been trying my best."

"Yes I've heard. That is a *young man* you have there, *cleaning*. I don't like it. I have had my differences with the boy, but now, after you, how will he be *fit*?" Mrs Purcell took a biscuit from the tin. Meredith sighed, picked up the suitcase and left. Then she went around to the back of the house, to the window behind which, curtains drawn, Henry seemed to be locked. Meredith tapped on the window. Henry stopped moaning and lifted a curtain. Meredith held up the suitcase, shook it a little, and then placed it below the window. Henry's eyebrows said thank you and Meredith went back to her house to work on finishing Mr Austen's manuscript.

"DO YOU WANT TO DIE in the stars, or in the sands?"

Henry could not have answered if he had wanted to, for he had been gagged with a black georgette scarf with golden tassels. It was balled at its base and its tentacles fluttered, some of which were stuck in Henry's nose.

Henry's eyes widened at the question. He had been jumped backstage while putting away the new jackets before meeting

Cathleen outside.

"Two choices," more pressure on Henry's chest, someone sitting on his chest cavity. With a pair of bare feet tickling his sides. A slight bouncing up and down made Henry's eyes close and his mouth open. "Two choices Henry: the stars..." waiting for a nod, a squeeze of the legs, a shudder. But Henry was frozen by the pain, "or the sand..." Again nothing from Henry. His chin needed a shave, it was so dry that skin was starting to peel. Breathing down on Henry's eyes, breath full of dates and wine boiled with cardamom seeped under Henry's eyelids. "Let me explain it to you then. Are you listening?" Henry's eyes relaxed, his mouth bit again on the gag, which now seemed cold and stale. Henry was listening. "If I send you to the stars, it means you will become so light that you will float off the floor and never return. You will feel this lightness because your insides will be removed and placed beside you, handful by handful, starting deep down here," laughter. Tightly pinching the skin covering Henry's stomach, as if trying to break into it, deep inside, "and then we move up, slowly, scoop by scoop, and you float, float up humbly to the stars. I do not pretend it will not be painful for you, Henry, and I would not really want it to be painless, not if I'm honest. You've really have had your fun, I have to say, with that slut of a whore."

Henry felt the cold stones underneath his back, buttocks and thighs. Two naked feet, previously only playing with his flanks, dug in with their toes extended, hard, rigid and probing for the mush inside Henry's guts. "Or you can choose the sands, Henry. That is your second choice. There was a beach, if you did not know, a beach of sand brought here to lay these stones upon. And it is to this beach I will send you, through the cracks of this floor until there is nothing left. I will do this by placing a great weight upon you, which, over a number of years, although again I do not kid myself into thinking that you will be around for all of them, but over a number of years this great weight will push your dissolving self down into the inland beach. And there you will be kept, under the stones, perhaps to come out and haunt my ancestors? Who knows? They can go to hell for all I care. But you, my dear Henry, you will be sent down below. A trip I will not make quick, for I will use, as the initial weight, a large wine vat. I will roll this vat over you with the greatest of care so that each bubble of your blood will be able to burst, to pop, to crowd upward toward your brain. So which is it, Henry, the sand or the stars? I want to know, please. Or else I can make the decision for you, which would be easy, for, if you cannot tell already, I would choose the sand. It just sounds so much more... intricate," at which a woman came up behind Captain Cooke and divested his head from his neck with a guard's sabre. The Captain's body fell off of Henry. Henry automatically started breathing deeply again. He had not yet understood what had happened when the woman began kissing Henry on the forehead, hands and heart. In that order, repeatedly.

MEREDITH'S FIRST TASK that afternoon was to see which of Mr Austen's papers she would look through first. She started to leaf through the pages which seemed like they were covered in poetry. Each page had one or two short bursts of inspiration and each had a title. They seemed to be a bunch of hymns, or songs, covering a wide range of topics: cosmology, myths, and history ancient and modern. Some of the titles were: 'Revolt of the Titans', 'The Virgin Mary', 'Clocks', 'Discovery of America', 'Luther', 'Shakespeare', 'Chiron', 'Uranium', 'Empedocles', 'Picasso', 'Battle of Hastings' and 'Hitler'. There were over a hundred poems because many of the sheets had more than one poem on them, and some of the poems were only two lines long. The whole project, whatever it was, sounded a bit grand to Meredith. But then again, she was not versed in poetry like Mr Austen. Meredith set the blue-poetry pile down and moved onto what was to become her first project, the pages in prose.

These pages seemed to make up a biography, the biography Meredith had hoped to find. Due to meeting the Purcells in France, Mr Austen started working on a biography of 17th-century composer Henry Purcell. About 30 manuscript pages had been written.

Meredith put all the other papers away in the lower right drawer of her dresser, the drawer containing postcards and sweaters. Then she sat down on the floor, to the right of the bed, facing the headboard, and laid the prose before her. She started reading through the first page, which started with a scene with the young Henry being led to some sort of cell. When she turned the page, because the papers had gotten all shuffled out of order when she dumped them out of the suitcase, she found that the story was more than a bit jumbled. So, smiling to herself, Meredith took a notebook from the kitchen drawer, padded back to the bedroom in her bare feet, sat down and inserted one blank page in between each page of Mr Austen's original text. "Now all I have to do is connect the dots," she thought. She took a pencil and began to do so, to write scenes connecting each scene written by Mr Austen. In this way she completed the biography of Henry Purcell.

MRS PURCELL ADJUSTED HER BLOUSE while sitting down. Her legs never crossed and the rough cotton of her skirt seemed to prick holes in Meredith's couch. Meredith really did not have time for this. For tea. She really was not in the mood.

Mrs Purcell had interrupted Meredith in the middle of her writing. Martino being absent, Meredith served tea herself.

"Oh, thank you dear," said Mrs Purcell.

"Yes, well. There you are."

"I just had to tell you."

"Yes," said Meredith, coming out of herself for a moment,

"you do look distressed. Whatever is it?"

"It's Henry. He's been captured."

"Captured!"

"Detained."

"Detained?"

"On the seaside, Calais. Boat to America from there. Hasn't even left France yet."

"But it's been months."

"Yes, you're right, it has. And I have you to thank for it. You and that Mr Austen. I wished we had never met the likes of you. Filling Henry's mind with such crazy thoughts. I never. I just wish that Henry and I had remained alone. And that I had never got ill. And most importantly that you would have kept your hussy self at home." At this Mrs Purcell stood up and left the room, her tea untested.

"EVELYN IS DEAD. Before attacking you, the Captain threw her into the river. But she didn't die right away. She dragged herself up onto the riverbank, just to die from the cold."

Cathleen sat down on the stone floor, next to where Henry was catching his breath.

"You... killed the Captain?" asked Henry, opening his eyes for the first time after passing out after the attack.

Cathleen smoothed her skirt out along the ground and stared at Henry. He looked at her in silence, but did not turn away. Then she put a finger under her nose in imitation of Henry's moustache. Henry, no matter how hard he tried, could not remain unstirred.

HENRY WAS STILL TRAPPED in Calais. Martino has received a letter, but it did not say much. Just that he was in need of clean linen. Martino brought the letter over to Meredith's for her to read. She tried reading the letter but was crying too much to make it out. Martino adjusted his shirt collar so that both tips sat flat underneath his sweater. He sat straight up in Meredith's plaid pillowed wicker chair on the other side of the coffee table. He was just about to touch his tea with his pinkie to see if it was yet drinkable. Meredith wiped her eyes and crossed her legs, twisting her whole body in Martino's direction.

Martino looked both at home and completely strange at the same time. He was back where he had been many times before, in the chair, sitting across from Meredith, about to have his tea, as if he had just finished the cleaning. But now things were different. He hadn't been in her house in months, and now this letter had brought him there again. Meredith was writing the Purcell biography, and Henry was in trouble in Calais.

"Disgusting," said Martino.

"Disgusting that they still have our Henry?" asked Meredith.

"Disgusting that they took him in the first place, that they are keeping him locked up in some dark cell. Disgusting that he's in trouble. It's all disgusting." Martino looked at his pinkie, nodded slightly to himself, and brought the cup up to his lips.

"Did you see him before he left?"

"I can't believe it," Martino said, ignoring her, "months and months in there. I can't imagine. We should really do something. Get him out. Hide him here." Then Martino's attention was distracted by the aroma of ginger coming from his saucer. "Hey, where did you manage to get this tea?"

"Laura," she said, trying not to say more, but unable. "She sent it when she heard I was working on the biography. She said she would be glad if her brother's name were left off it. That's her idea."

Martino seemed to hardly hear her as he rushed through his cup of tea. Meredith, knowing Martino never had a second, at least had never wanted a second before, thought now that maybe he would. She hesitated filling her own cup, giving him a chance to ask for another. But Martino said nothing. Then she set the pot back down next to the tea cozy and asked, "Well, do you want to see it?"

Martino's eyes narrowed. "Excuse me?"

"The postcard. The horse. The reason for all this. Do you want to see it?"

Martino looked down into his tea cup, which he held with both hands, seemingly mesmerized as he swirled the remaining dregs.

"I have it right there, in my bedroom. In the dresser. Lower right-hand corner. With the sweaters. You can get it if you want. Or I could bring it out to you here in the living room. Would you like that?"

Martino stopped swirling but did not look up from the tea cup.

"I could leave the house for a while. Or put it outside somewhere for you to find, maybe buried, in a handkerchief or something, near the pavement on the way in? Then you could find it there whenever you want. It would not even have to be today. But don't wait too long, because of the rain. But it hasn't rained for weeks, so you should be all right, even if you wait a bit. Or I could just bring it to you now... I'm just trying to be helpful," said Meredith, not daring to brush her hair out of her eyes.

Martino poured himself another cup of tea. "Maybe outside, then," he said.

Meredith let herself smile, stood up from the couch, went into the bedroom, took the postcards out of her drawer, and set them on fire.

Epilogue

1

Slower than fast slow
moderated downward
shuffle past first idling
super-hot water kicks
out and round racehorses
once again out of gate —
emitting continued neutrons,
pressure melting syntax
cooling condensing wet hot
powers a city of millions.

* * *

Back and forth,
a combination lock
quick set zero burnt snapped dial spun
mismatched socks open drawer smeared shadow
carpet strewn brown.
Discs slip into drives heads into hats laps thighs
a cable under the ocean dropped by seamen chaffing,
carrying countless fading letters and lovers
wind battering it must come up somewhere — the cable
twisted one wire for each letter sputters out the surface
dry land saps, pencil pusher pushed
a second atom split in a cold cold country.

* * *

Oh to turn me out
right not quite there yet
not quite there
rich black blends in quick

with water too heavy to carry
shoulders too woman to hold
action we need action down here —
for all we are are the halflives
fizzling the sweetest of sweet spots.

2

Hard-held heaven burst its only flame
downward, spilling pews purple lost in prayer.
Two young bathers up from the shore
excelling their gross game
there, at the altar, fixed forms floored
wood angles crack, fighting and bored —
polished speech, creatures run
not ready, not caring —
springing seashore awaits the cutting fingers shaking
the bed you need resting out long before them both.

3

On horse or donkey in the desert
in front of a gate encased in stone
black bent twists wide gaps filter
only the largest of debris escape,
except this gate is already open
tight sand making glass against
the wall, filter flat against door —
letting trash from courtyards within
out, scuttling past the four legs waiting
for a command from Meredith riding.

The doorkeeper's shadow quivers,
grainy hard against sand-packed stone
rising up and keeping sand at bay —
the shadow aware of the woman at the gate,
the gate aware of its doing no good,
the horse or donkey, aware,
Meredith holding its reins
in both hands tightly, knowing the shadows
on the other side are nervous
with desire to have everyone
stay on their side.

A key unused in right-flank saddlebag
a message folded in left-breast pocket
reins unsnapped in rough-gloved hands —
unfaded gate unclosed, walls left uncrumbled
a dust line backed up behind her, waiting
to sail through the gate into the city —
dust curling in and over through the desert
lifting tail and approaching the behind
spinning up hindlegs sandburn reddens,

angry at being stalled so far from home.

All around the desert is empty except
men hanging up pictures in halls except
women dancing on tables except
fires breeding in drunk wine except
children staying up late except
pigs pleading with their ghosts except
priests fumbling with pages except
classes held by candlelight except

There are too many crenels on the wall
to see what makes each one unique —
follow the patters of cracks, wear and chips
up over down over and up either,
too much asperity or none at all
tiny black holes between tiny sand grains —
far too many grains behind those holes,
or maybe they can be counted and catalogued
like Linnaeus naming *Zingiber officinale*
after the Sanskrit for shaped like a horn,

which ginger is, just like sand packed tight
in walls rising up its sides
like nervous hooves burning
and not like cold keys and limp reins
or unused shadows and open gates
or a latent gallop, a mighty whinny —
too many grains mean too much
to be discounted, too quickly,
each one had a purpose before
being encased in its crack.

Meredith, steadfast,

a hole or a grain, a key or
a gate, a horse or a donkey,
inside or outside the city,
a filter for trash or an uneasy portal —
mistakes counted on both sides.

Her, outside the city and outside the desert
a blueprint for the creation of new starts
an echo between falling grains of sand
a stress holding walls too heavy to fathom
although each kilo, its weight behind it,
tugging constantly down
pockets of echo a salve for holes filled
grains bruised on their way up
rations tightened, troops in formation
nothing is random when you're under attack.

The horse or donkey coughs,
sand, working frontwards,
thickening spittle hardening between teeth
coming out in spurts and sprays —
Meredith from right flank saddlebag removes
two quarts of tightly-packed milk
and dismounting administers
the pacifying, twisting stream
to tooth and eye and throat
of donkey or horse and shadow.

Acknowledgements

Thank you to Peter Greenaway for agreeing to the use of suitcase #55, "Clean Linen," from his *Tulse Luper Suitcases*, as the original impetus for this project. Although *Henry, Henry* has undergone many revisions since then, traces of Greenaway remain in the clothes, imprisonment and uranium found in the story. In addition, apologies are due to Sir Jack Westrup for the misappropriation and blatant disregard of his *Purcell* (New York: J.M. Dent and Sons, 1937).

Zero Books
CULTURE, SOCIETY & POLITICS

Contemporary culture has eliminated the concept and public figure of the intellectual. A cretinous anti-intellectualism presides, cheer-led by hacks in the pay of multinational corporations who reassure their bored readers that there is no need to rouse themselves from their stupor. Zer0 Books knows that another kind of discourse - intellectual without being academic, popular without being populist - is not only possible: it is already flourishing. Zer0 is convinced that in the unthinking, blandly consensual culture in which we live, critical and engaged theoretical reflection is more important than ever before.

If you have enjoyed this book, why not tell other readers by posting a review on your preferred book site. Recent bestsellers from Zero Books are:

In the Dust of This Planet
Horror of Philosophy vol. 1
Eugene Thacker
In the first of a series of three books on the Horror of Philosophy, In the Dust of This Planet offers the genre of horror as a way of thinking about the unthinkable.
Paperback: 978-1-84694-676-9 ebook: 978-1-78099-010-1

Capitalist Realism
Is there no alternative?
Mark Fisher
An analysis of the ways in which capitalism has presented itself as the only realistic political-economic system.
Paperback: 978-1-84694-317-1 ebook: 978-1-78099-734-6

Rebel Rebel
Chris O'Leary
David Bowie: every single song. Everything you want to know, everything you didn't know.
Paperback: 978-1-78099-244-0 ebook: 978-1-78099-713-1

Cartographies of the Absolute
Alberto Toscano, Jeff Kinkle
An aesthetics of the economy for the twenty-first century.
Paperback: 978-1-78099-275-4 ebook: 978-1-78279-973-3

Malign Velocities
Accelerationism and Capitalism
Benjamin Noys
Long listed for the Bread and Roses Prize 2015, Malign Velocities argues against the need for speed, tracking acceleration as the symptom of the on-going crises of capitalism.
Paperback: 978-1-78279-300-7 ebook: 978-1-78279-299-4

Meat Market
Female flesh under Capitalism
Laurie Penny
A feminist dissection of women's bodies as the fleshy fulcrum of capitalist cannibalism, whereby women are both consumers and consumed.
Paperback: 978-1-84694-521-2 ebook: 978-1-84694-782-7

Poor but Sexy
Culture Clashes in Europe East and West
Agata Pyzik
How the East stayed East and the West stayed West.
Paperback: 978-1-78099-394-2 ebook: 978-1-78099-395-9

Romeo and Juliet in Palestine
Teaching Under Occupation
Tom Sperlinger
Life in the West Bank, the nature of pedagogy and the role of a
university under occupation.
Paperback: 978-1-78279-637-4 ebook: 978-1-78279-636-7

Sweetening the Pill
or How we Got Hooked on Hormonal Birth Control
Holly Grigg-Spall
Has contraception liberated or oppressed women? *Sweetening
the Pill* breaks the silence on the dark side of hormonal
contraception.
Paperback: 978-1-78099-607-3 ebook: 978-1-78099-608-0

Why Are We The Good Guys?
Reclaiming your Mind from the Delusions of Propaganda
David Cromwell
A provocative challenge to the standard ideology that Western
power is a benevolent force in the world.
Paperback: 978-1-78099-365-2 ebook: 978-1-78099-366-9

Readers of ebooks can buy or view any of these bestsellers by
clicking on the live link in the title. Most titles are published in
paperback and as an ebook. Paperbacks are available in traditional
bookshops. Both print and ebook formats are available online.

Find more titles and sign up to our readers' newsletter at
http://www.johnhuntpublishing.com/culture-and-politics.
Follow us on Facebook at https://www.facebook.com/ZeroBooks
and Twitter at https://twitter.com/Zer0Books.